DEATH
IN THE
SPIRIT HOUSE

also by Craig Strete

DEATH CHANTS

DREAMS THAT BURN IN THE NIGHT

IF ALL ELSE FAILS . . .

DEATH
IN THE
SPIRIT HOUSE

CRAIG · STRETE

A FOUNDATION BOOK

Doubleday

NEW YORK LONDON TORONTO SYDNEY

All of the characters in this book
are fictitious, and any resemblance
to actual persons, living or dead,
is purely coincidental.

A Foundation Book
Published by Doubleday, a division of
Bantam Doubleday Dell Publishing Group, Inc.,
666 Fifth Avnue, New York, New York 10103

Foundation and the portrayal of the letter F
are trademarks of Doubleday, a division of
Bantam Doubleday Dell Publishing Group, Inc.

DESIGNED BY VIRGINIA M. SOULÉ

Library of Congress Cataloging-in-Publication Data
Strete, Craig.
Death in the spirit house/Craig Strete.
p.   cm.
1. Indians of North America—Fiction.   I. Title.
PS3569.T6935D45   1988
813'.54—dc19   87-35209
                                                                            CIP

ISBN 0-385-17826-3
Copyright © 1988 by Craig Strete
All Rights Reserved
Printed in the United States of America
First Edition
July 1988

BG

DEATH
IN THE
SPIRIT HOUSE

1

Solomon Hawk stared at his wife. His eyes were unrelenting.

"It must be done, woman."

The old, gray-haired woman sat rocking in her chair. Her eyes were closed. Her long braids touched the arms of the chair. Lianna Hawk opened her eyes slowly and her eyes sought those of her husband.

"He is our son," she said simply.

"Once I called him my son. Not anymore."

"He is of our flesh, of our bones and blood. You must not do this thing." The old woman closed her eyes, settling back against the hard back of her rocker. She seemed in that moment to be a thousand years old. She knew her argument was useless.

The old man dropped an armful of clothes on the table. He was angry, but in a sorrowful way. "I have spoken my mind and the wind blows only one way through this valley. This one I once called son is evil. A killer. Of men. Of the sacred animals of this earth. His heart is black. He kills for the joy of it. I will not have his spirit in this house."

"It is true, husband," said Lianna sadly, an ache in her voice. "He has no respect for life. Nothing is sacred to him. But is it our path to punish him? Someday the bad death he has earned will come for him. It watches him and someday it will come for him."

"Let it find him somewhere else. I do not know his name. I wish him dead in my heart. Nothing of his shall be in this house," said the old man, bitterness in his voice.

"Old age has made you unforgiving."

"No. It has made me see only what is . . . not what the inside of me wants to see. I have no more dreams or visions but I know the world that moves between my hands."

The old man scooped up the load of clothes and took it outside. He walked to a battered old car that stood beside the shack. The car was loaded down with clothes, animal pelts, rifles and other kinds of things. Everything in the car belonged to his son, Red Hawk. The car was Red Hawk's too.

The old man went back into the house. The old woman got up from her chair. She set a small brown box on the battered table.

The old man stared at the box.

Lianna stood behind the table. There was pain in her eyes. "Would you throw this away too?"

"That too." The old man balled his hands into fists, dug them into his sides as if angry at himself.

"You were proud of these once. In the town you went among the men and made proud boasts of your son to them."

"I remember, woman." The old man looked tired, very tired. "Give it to me." He held out his hand. "I was a fool, woman. A fool to think him capable of anything worth praising to others."

She opened the box and took out two military medals wrapped in a faded newspaper clipping. "Do you want me to read you this clipping, this newspaper writing about the bravery of our son?" The old woman sounded bitter.

The old man did not withdraw his hand. "It says he killed ten of the enemy. That he went in under fire at the risk of his own life and carried Sheriff Fiske's son out of danger. I know what it says."

"It does not fill you with pride? It does not fill your heart?" The old woman wiped tears from the corners of her eyes. Her back sagged as if under a heavy weight. She seemed ready to collapse.

"Woman, what it says and what he did . . . these things are two different things. He did not tell you that Sheriff Fiske's boy was shot by his own commander. He did not tell you that he and his friend had killed innocent children, not ten enemy soldiers, and that they were caught in this vileness by their own commander."

"You"—the old woman was stunned—"you make this all up! . . . It's lies! . . . Lies! It says right here in this paper writing!" The old woman held tightly to the clipping.

"One night when they were drunk, both just come home from the Vietnam War, they told me everything. They thought it was a very funny thing. Leonard Fiske and Red Hawk were drunk right here in this house and I was making a fool of myself in my pride of them. They had returned warriors and I was proud of them."

"As should be."

"They did not let me enjoy it very long. They told me everything. They laughed at me. They said I was a stupid old man. Red Hawk killed his commander and two men who were with him. It was not the enemy that killed them as it says in the newspaper writing. They did it themselves to keep from going to Army prison."

The old woman closed her eyes and leaned against the table. She knew Solomon would not lie, had never lied.

She stiffened her back, stood up tall. Her eyes opened wide and she stared down at the medals and the newspaper clipping in her hand.

She held them out abruptly to the old man. "Don't forget these. They are lies brought into this house by some stranger. I will not have shame in this house."

The old man took the medals from her hand. His hand caught hers for a moment and caressed it. The old woman met his eyes with her own. Tears ran down her cheeks. "You have always been my strength," said the old man.

"And you mine," she answered.

"Come help me burn the memories of two old fools who once had a son," he said. They moved with the sadness of the defeated.

Together they went outside the house. Solomon threw the medals in the car.

The old woman got a can of gasoline and began pouring it on the car. She rolled down a car window and poured some inside. She poured some on the ground behind the car.

When the gas can was empty, the old man made her step back.

Solomon picked up a bundle of dried grass and held it out to her. She lit one end of it with a match. The dry grass ignited at once, sending up heavy white smoke. It burned rapidly.

The old man swung it over his shoulder and let it go. It blazed like a meteor and hit the car.

The car exploded in a brilliant orange fireball, driving the old people back with the sheer intensity of the heat.

Red Hawk was no longer of their house, or of their flesh.

They had burned him out of their lives.

There were others who would burn him as well.

At that very moment, Red Hawk sat in the local jail, a prisoner of the man whose son he had supposedly saved in Vietnam. He was awaiting a jury trial that would find him guilty. He'd shot a woman in a bar because she said he was a bastard. She died in a pool of blood at his feet. Drunk, he had laughed and challenged anybody else to call him a bastard.

The bartender had hit him from behind with a blackjack and Red Hawk woke up in jail the next morning. If he had any regrets, it was probably only that he had not shot the bartender too.

The old people went back inside the house. They sat in their chairs beside the fireplace and the silence closed in on them in their sorrow like a fist.

The old man broke the silence finally. "The only thing I do not understand . . . the thing that worries me." He shook his head. "This mountain is sacred to our people and the animals that live on it are sacred. Our people hunted only in the valleys, for it was known that all of the animal people that lived in the high places belonged to the spirit of the mountain. But Red Hawk broke the ancient ways. Taking those dressed-up white men into the mountains to kill our mountain sheep, the whitetail, cougar and bear. He himself killed the sacred animals for bounty, not even for food. Yet he escapes the anger of the mountain. I do not understand how this can be so."

"You think the mountain has forgotten him, that Red Hawk will escape the mountain's revenge?" asked the old woman. "I have felt the heart of this mountain more deeply than you and I say it waits for him. That it will call him one final time and it will take his life."

"He will die in the electric chair," said Solomon.

"I wish him that easy death," said Lianna, and her eyes went past him and came to rest on the mountain rising above their cabin. "But the death the mountain spins for him will match all the evil of his life. I know it in my heart. It will not be denied its pleasure."

The old man shuddered. Lianna had a way of knowing things that was past his understanding. The old man went to the door.

"It is done, then. He is gone from our lives. We still have his horse and the new colt it's given birth to. We will give them away. I would not see them killed," he said, but it was not to be.

2

The mountain towered above a sea of pines. Hidden rivers ran through its stone heart. A lonely cabin in a clearing clung to the mountain at the edge of the timberline. The mountain's proud face was scarred with its centuries.

The white people who came later had a name for it, but the real people who came first knew the mountain's true and everlasting name. They called it Spirit House.

The mountain was a woman. Mighty hands had painted her face and put her between the great sea and the oceans of sand and wind. The spirit of this mighty mountain was a thing of awesome power and as with all things beyond understanding it was a creature of the nightland, a thing of secrets and terrible passions. The spirit of the mountain burned through the night of its life with a strange and terrible beauty.

Spirit House was fashioned out of a great mystery and none could tame her, none could truly possess her.

It was said by the real people that the animals that walked her slopes, those that lived upon her broad back in the high places, were like no other animals in the world. The real people said these animals were created by the woman spirit of the mountain, that they might love her.

It was known that she loved them, deer, bear, snake, lizard, all the creatures of the mountain, for it was said that she dealt unkindly with those who hurt or killed those animals she loved. None of the real people ever hunted there. Spirit House and her animals were sacred.

There were those to whom the mountain was not sacred, to whom nothing was sacred. Spirit House awaited their coming.

She had the power to heal and the power to kill.

The lone cabin in the clearing high up the mountain belonged to two of the real people, old in their years and wise in the ways of their kind, Solomon Hawk and Lianna, his wife. In a log corral near the weather-beaten shack a handsome mare paced. The horse belonged to the son of the two who lived in the cabin.

It was a beautiful day. Morning flowers, coaxed by the sun, pushed through the patchy snow.

In the thorn tangles on the low hill near the clearing something moved. Something that moved quietly through the tangled underbrush. The tops of the bushes stirred, but only the chirping birds and the hum of the insects could be heard.

The mare swished her tail nervously. The awkward-looking colt with the spindly legs of the newborn tossed his head and moved in to nurse. The mare whickered then, aware of some presence outside the corral. The colt whinnied impatiently, butting its mother to get her to stand still. The colt was oblivious to all but its own hunger.

From the hill another sound intruded on the everyday sounds of birds and insects. It was a harsh, rasping sound of something breathing, something big and well hidden. The source of the sound moved closer, leaving a wake of shifting branches.

The presence gained the low ground and moved into the trees along the edge of the clearing.

A thin wisp of smoke rose from the stone chimney alongside the ramshackle cabin. The front door was partially ajar. Behind the cabin the hulk of a burned-out car rested. Whatever had happened to the car had happened recently. The car still smoldered, sending acrid black fumes into the air.

The sound of voices, those of a man and a woman, drifted out the open doorway. The words carried clearly across the clearing.

The woman was saying, "And I say the mountain will deliver a sign. It will draw Red Hawk like a fly into its web."

If the presence hidden in the trees heard or understood, it gave no sign.

The mare bolted forward, knocking the colt aside. The mare was terrified.

Outside, in the trees, something moved again, coming closer. A long shadow fell over the spring snow that quilted the clearing. The wind shifted and some smell, the scent of something lurking in the trees, clearly reached the nervous mare.

The mare rose on her hind legs, flailing at the sky as she whinnied in terror. At the sound of her scream, the shadow in the trees galvanized into a blur of motion.

The thing that sped across the clearing was the enameled ebony of a moonless night. Its powerful charge carried it across the clearing in two bounds.

It was nearly fourteen feet long from exposed fangs to the tip of its tail. It weighed over seven hundred pounds.

It was a cougar, black as sin, and none like it had ever walked the face of this earth.

The big cat hit the ground in front of the corral and did not break stride as it soared into the air, clearing the man-high logs by a good four feet. The panicked mare pivoted on its hind legs, striking out with slashing forehooves.

The mare had no chance. The razor-sharp claws sank into the doomed horse's sides as the murderous jaws closed on the back of its neck. Arterial blood geysered into the air. The impact of the cat slammed the horse to the ground, its flanks ripped and bloody.

Solomon rose up from his chair. His wife was at his side. Both heard the sounds of a disturbance coming from the corral. Solomon went to the wall and took his old rifle off the pegs above the fireplace. "Sounds like trouble."

The horse screamed in terror.

Solomon started for the door, but his wife stepped in front of him, putting her hand on the rifle. "It's a mountain animal. You cannot shoot it."

"I can scare it. Might be a cougar looking for a nice tasty colt."

"I'm coming too," she said.

He ran out the door, loading the gun as he went. She followed closely behind. They turned the corner of the cabin and stopped dead at the rails of the corral. They arrived just as the cat struck the horse again.

The cat jerked its head once, its jaws locked into the mare's neck. There was a snap like dry wood breaking and the head separated from the body.

The tiny colt was frozen in terror against the far side of the enclosure.

The cat stretched out in the dust beside the dead mare. It did not touch the dead horse, did not even nose the fresh meat in front of it. It looked up at the two old people standing at the corral rails. Its eyes glared calmly at them.

The old man slowly raised the rifle. The cat did not move. In all of his years upon this world, the old man had never seen a black cougar. He'd seen them brown, yellowish, mottled, all kinds of colors. Never black. He'd heard of them but never seen one. And never had he seen a cougar this size. His hands trembled as he held the rifle. No cougar ever got that big. Never.

At sight of the raised rifle, the cat growled, a deep-throated rumble that echoed across the clearing.

Solomon brought the gun down slowly until he held it in both hands.

Lianna leaned against him, terrified. "Don't shoot!" she said. "This great black one belongs to Spirit House."

"I can't let him kill the colt," said Solomon. "I'll just scare him off."

With shaking hands, the old man pumped the lever, ramming a shell into the chamber. As the lever reached its down position, it made a *click.*

The sound was a small thing in the mountain air, but the cat heard it. It stood up, bared its fangs.

Solomon fired in the air.

The cat did not run. It stepped over the body of the dead horse and walked toward the colt. In its terror, the colt tried to press itself through the hard wooden rails of the corral. The cat stared at the colt, snarled and turned its back on it.

The cat spun and looked at the old people. Its hard yellow eyes burned into them. Suddenly it gathered itself together and sailed over the corral rails, clearing them by at least a yard. The black cougar broke left, making for the trees with express-train speed.

The black form crashed into the heavy brush and disappeared from sight.

Solomon stood there, holding the useless rifle, and stared into the trees where the big cat had gone.

His wife took the gun out of his nerveless hands. "Go into town. Tell the sheriff what has happened. Red Hawk will come with him."

The old man was trembling. "What are you talking about? Red Hawk is in jail for murder! They'll never let him out."

"Do what I say," said the old woman, ejecting the spent cartridge. The old woman seemed as hard as the stone of the mountain. Her voice was as cold as a mountain wind. "The mountain has called for him. If there is a way for him to come, he will come. No jail will stop him from answering the call of Spirit House."

The old woman turned ashen and gray. It was as if winter had seized upon her soul. "I feel it in my bones, the terrible thing that walks out there and must be answered."

The old man turned away from the corral. "I'll go." He tried not to, but his eyes kept returning to the severed head of the mare lying in a pool of its own blood. "It did not even eat. Just killed. My shot did not even scare it," he said. There was a fine edge of terror in his voice.

"Go," said the old woman. "We owe it to the mountain. We owe nothing to our son."

3

NORTHPASS COLORADO
POPULATION 4453
ELEVATION 9000

The sign flashed by as the battered pickup swerved and careened down a two-lane road twisting through the hills. Solomon Hawk gripped the steering wheel hard and stared out the cracked windshield at the sign he had seen too many times before. The look on his face was grim.

Northpass was an ugly blemish amid the splendors of Spirit House mountain. It was not much more than a collection of buildings flanking the road, a town tucked into the sides of a high mountain pass. The highway was its main street, its only street in fact.

A motor court that catered to the winter skiers sprawled on the edge of town, its battered vacancy sign swinging in the wind.

Up the street, a bank, a movie theater and several bars made up the center of town. Solomon's eyes mechanically catalogued these facts as he drove through town.

Most of the businesses were closed for the season.

In the jail, toward which Solomon was headed, two men sat at a round wooden table playing cards.

Deputy Sheriff Lloyd Fiske scowled at his cards and threw them down in disgust. He reached behind the sunglasses clipped to his uniform shirt pocket, fished out several coins.

He dropped them on the table and reluctantly pushed them forward toward another pile of coins that rested in front of the other man.

Fiske was gray-haired, lean with a hard body that age had yet to line with fat. He was tall, slightly built almost.

Red Hawk smiled and raked in the change. He was a startling contrast to the other man. Hampered by the handcuffs, Red Hawk began to shuffle the cards to the country music rhythms blaring from a small black radio at his elbow.

Red Hawk was big, massive, with thick coal-black hair tumbling down past his broad shoulders. His face was harsh and of a bitter cast. He resembled a man hewn from flint. He wore combat boots, a ripped deerskin shirt and faded blue Levi's bleached almost white by the sun.

On the corded muscles of his arms were several crudely lettered tattoos, obviously done by himself. His huge hands, thick and callused, made the playing cards look like postage stamps as they tumbled off his thick fingers.

"Your son and me, we really had us a time in Vietnam," said Red Hawk, offering the cards for a cut. "I've hunted everything there is to hunt, wolf, elk, bear and deer. But hunting man is best of all."

Fiske scowled and cut the cards. He found the subject uncomfortable.

"I heard from Leonard yesterday. He's not coming home," said Fiske. "It wasn't just losing the leg. His mind is gone too. He's never going to come back from the Vietnam War."

"He's one of the lucky ones," said Red Hawk, dealing out the first card. "If he lost his mind, he's got nothing to remember. Dead would be best, but crazy is a good second. I don't remember much of my life before Vietnam. It seems like it didn't happen. I'm just one mean son of a bitch now."

"You were always a son of a bitch," said Fiske. "Vietnam just made you a full-time professional son of a bitch."

"I was good at soldiering," said Red Hawk defensively. "I got the medals to prove it. Say, did I ever tell you about the time Leonard and me came on a patrol of Vietcong getting themselves set into position for an ambush. He and I were on point for a recon patrol. We had made a kind of loop in front of the recon and came out in back of the Cong. There was eight of them.

"Old Leonard says, 'Bet you I can take out all eight of them before they can get off a shot.'

" 'A carton of cigarettes says you can't,' I tell him.

"So Leonard opens fire. Intermittent bursts. Pops two with no trouble. Real sweet. He's really chopping them up and then his gun jams and he's got big trouble.

"Suddenly there's six jaybirds hammering at him with all they got. The air is so full around his head he could breathe lead.

"I'm sitting behind a tree, laughing fit to burst a gut. Leonard dives behind my tree, near lands in my lap!

" 'Well, Leonard,' I says, 'did they get off a shot there now, Leonard?' "

Red Hawk burst out laughing at the memory.

Fiske rested his hands on his balled fists, not smiling.

"Then there was the time we saw a Vietcong up in a tree asleep. So I bet Leonard that . . ."

Fiske pushed his hat back on his head. "Just shut up and deal."

Red Hawk laughed and dealt out two cards to each of them.

"What's the matter, Sheriff? Where's the old patriotic spirit? Don't killing Commies interest you?" asked Red Hawk.

"I don't like killing, period," said Fiske. "I don't like hunting animals any more than I like hunting men." He frowned at the cards Red Hawk had dealt him. "And you're not going to be interested much longer yourself after the jury gets through with you. So shut up and play cards."

"No respect for a war vet? Christ! Bleeding hearts are ruining everything," said Red Hawk, ignoring Fiske. "Just like hunting. Goddamn, there used to be good hunting up there on Spirit House mountain. Rest of the tribe was too scared to hunt up there. The old tribal superstitions kept them away. A lot of scared old women, if you ask me." He glanced at his cards and smiled. He continued. "Then the damn government takes the bounty off the big cats and cuts down the white-tailed deer season. Ruined one hell of a sweet deal I had going. Used to get the white boys from out of town to pay for a cougar-hunting trip, then I'd turn the heads in myself and get the government bounty. Bounty money and guide money! Christ! Guess I killed my share of cougars and whitetails up on Spirit House. Damn government!"

Fiske held his cards between two fingers and frowned.

"You gonna talk about how hard life is and show me your baby pictures or are you gonna play cards?" He scowled. "Hit me!"

Red Hawk slid another card to Fiske across the tabletop.

"Again."

Red Hawk tossed another card.

"Busted," said Fiske, throwing in his cards.

"I stood on thirteen," said Red Hawk, picking up the pot, enjoying the triumph.

"Damn," said Fiske. "And I went and hit on sixteen!"

Red Hawk dealt another hand and the game went on.

Outside, Solomon's pickup truck skidded around the corner and came to a screeching halt in front of the building. Red Hawk looked up, startled. His father got out of the cab of the truck and hobbled toward the jail.

"Here comes my old man, in one hell of a hurry. He must have to take a leak." Red Hawk frowned. "Now why the hell would he be coming here? He can't stand my guts."

Fiske studied his cards, ignoring the commotion outside. He finally looked up as Solomon stormed through the door.

Sheriff Fiske could see that Solomon was upset, deeply troubled about something.

"You come to see Red Hawk?" asked Fiske, surprised.

"Maybe," said Solomon, a strange expression on his face. "But mainly I came to see you."

Fiske dropped his cards on the table. "Well, you're seeing me. What can I do for you?"

Solomon spoke to Fiske but his eyes bored into Red Hawk's eyes. His son met his stare unflinchingly, defiantly.

"Red Hawk's got a prize mare and new colt stabled in back of our cabin. About half an hour ago, a black cougar, I'd guess all of fourteen feet long, paid us a visit. Killed the mare! Jumped the corral fence by a good four foot, I swear."

Red Hawk threw his cards down on the table, half rising from his seat. "What? Killed my mare? A black cougar and you say it's how big?" There was a look of disbelief on his face.

"Fourteen foot, maybe bigger."

Red Hawk angrily pushed his chair away from the table.

"You're half blind, old man. Are you sure it wasn't an enraged rooster mounting one of those scrawny pullets you keep out there in the chicken coop?"

Furious, Solomon turned on his son. "You will not say those words to me! I've told you what I saw. The horse is dead. The cougar bit its head off. It was big enough to do that. Come and see if you do not believe me!"

"Come off it!" said Red Hawk, moving his hands in a gesture of dismissal that made the handcuffs rattle against each other. "You've been drinking white lightning again, old man."

Fiske interrupted the argument. "Exactly what happened?" he asked.

Solomon shrugged. "What more is there to tell? Lianna and I were inside when we heard a commotion out in the corral. We had just been outside a few hours before, burning some . . . burning some . . . garbage." He looked at Red Hawk. "The horse and colt were fine then."

Solomon licked his lips nervously. He went on. "Later we heard the mare spook. By the time we got there, the black cougar had already jumped her. We were too late to do anything."

"A black cougar ripped up my mare?" said Red Hawk. "Son of a bitch! I want to see it!"

"I fired a warning shot to scare it off the colt but the cougar didn't seem interested in the colt. It didn't budge an inch when I fired my gun either. Left when it was good and ready, not a minute sooner."

"A black cougar," Red Hawk repeated, and he touched a thin white scar on his cheek, and for a few seconds was lost in some private thoughts of his own.

Deputy Sheriff Fiske unhooked his sunglasses from his shirt pocket and slid them over his eyes. He stood up, motioning Red Hawk toward the cell at the back of the room. "I'll put you away and go take a look. Hell, I was losing at cards anyway."

"Take me along," said Red Hawk. "It's my mare that got killed. I got a right to see it for myself!"

"You got a right to go in there, sit on your cell bunk and hope that somebody remembers to feed you." He gave Red Hawk a shove in the direction of the cell. Red Hawk didn't budge.

"It's my horse," declared Red Hawk. "I got a right to see it."

Solomon looked at Fiske, studying the sheriff to see what he would do. Fiske noticed the old man staring at him, noticed the curious, troubled expression on Solomon's face.

"Look! Goddamnit! I saved your son's life in Vietnam. That ought to count for something," said Red Hawk. "You can keep the damn cuffs on me. Come on! My word of honor I won't cause any trouble."

Solomon scowled and said, "You have no honor. How can you give your word on it?"

Red Hawk ignored him. "C'mon, Fiske. You haven't got anybody to watch me while you're gone, you gotta take me along. Let me get outside and get the stink blowed off. I don't get no exercise in here."

Red Hawk was as close to begging as he ever got.

Fiske looked at the cell, looked back at Solomon. "He's your son. You want him along or should I lock him up?"

Solomon turned pale and his hands shook. "I . . ." He rubbed the back of his hand across his mouth nervously. "I don't mind," he finally said.

As he spoke those words, he felt a heavy thing close over his soul. He was certain he had just delivered Red Hawk to his death, and a horrible one at that.

Fiske grabbed a rifle out of the rack on the wall, grabbed a box of cartridges. He herded Solomon and Red Hawk out the front door.

"Let's go see if this monster cat of yours left any sign," he said.

He tapped Red Hawk with the barrel of the rifle. "And you best behave," he cautioned, "or I'll have to put a hole in your hide and let you leak out all over the place."

4

The battered pickup rolled up the dirt road followed by a jeep bearing county markings. Red Hawk was handcuffed to the tailgate of the pickup so Fiske in the jeep behind could keep an eye on him. Red Hawk wasn't too happy about the arrangement.

Fiske steered the jeep over the rutted road, a rifle balanced lightly on his knees. Both vehicles ground to a stop in a cloud of thick dust in front of Solomon's cabin.

Fiske gave Solomon the key to unlock the handcuffs. Red Hawk was set free, then promptly had his hands fastened together in front of him again. Solomon did the task grimly, while Fiske kept the rifle trained on Red Hawk.

"Thanks, Father," said Red Hawk sarcastically. "What would I have done without your help?"

"Died early," said Solomon. "Of the wrong thing."

Fiske asked, "Where's your wife?"

"Lianna is staying in the cabin. She doesn't want to see Red Hawk," explained Solomon.

"Weak stomach?" asked Red Hawk.

Solomon pointed to a patch of snow beside the cabin. "There," he said, almost reverently.

In the center of the dirty white mound was a single paw print. Fiske knelt, keeping one eye always on Red Hawk. He pushed his hat back on his head and uttered a low whistle. "I'll be damned!"

Red Hawk came up beside them and bent down to look at the print. Even he was impressed. He went to his knees, awkward, with his hands bound together. He tilted his hands, placing one palm over the print that rested there. His own massive hand, fingers stretched wide, barely covered it.

"Goddamn!" Red Hawk was surprised. "This cougar's got to be twelve, thirteen feet at least."

"Fourteen," said Solomon. "And black as night."

Red Hawk jerked his head up, fixing his father with a hard stare.

"How black? Do you mean dark, mottled brown, dirty?"

"I mean black," repeated Solomon.

Red Hawk stiffened visibly. A strange look passed over his face. His hands balled into fists.

"Born and raised here, Solomon," said Fiske, gesturing at the surrounding mountains with his rifle. "Ain't never seen a black cougar. Course, never heard of one this big either."

Fiske turned and looked at Red Hawk.

"All that hunting you done round Spirit House, Red Hawk. You ever run a black cougar? Or hear tell of one?"

Red Hawk's hand went to his face, tracing a thin white scar that ran from under his chin to just below his right eye. He spoke very softly.

"Once, just once." He turned his back on them, his eyes on the slopes of Spirit House. Red Hawk found himself remembering something from four years ago. He had tracked a female cougar for three days and *that* cat had been smart. She knew he was there but for some reason she didn't take to the high ground. She just led him around in frustrating circles. As he peered through the rifle scope on the third day he had seen why.

There were two half-grown cubs. One was the same shade as the mother. The other was the bigger of the two. It was jet black. A black pelt ought to be worth a fortune. Hunters talked about them but finding one was a once-in-a-lifetime chance, they were that rare.

He had centered the cross hairs of the scope on the mother cat and squeezed the trigger. He loved the thunder of the gun booming under his shoulder, loved the first shudder of impact as the slug drove home. He was not disappointed. The 7 mm magnum slug caught her just under the right shoulder. The mushrooming effect of the hollow point burst her lungs and heart at the same time. She was dead before the sound of the shot reached her cubs. He'd laughed, pleased that he'd made such a good solid killing shot from that great a distance.

He'd pulled back the bolt and chambered another shell.

The two cubs were playing, unaware of the tragedy that had overtaken their mother.

Red Hawk's next shot had exploded the smaller cub. The black cub had looked around curiously and licked at its dead sibling's face.

Red Hawk had left the cover of the big rocks and zigzagged down the hillside toward the lone cub. The animal saw him and its fur rose along its spine but it did not leave its fallen family. It was almost half the size of its mother and Red Hawk had marveled at the sleekness of its black coat.

He tried for a head shot to preserve the pelt and the cat jerked and went down in the tall grass. As he approached the three bodies, the mother cougar was the nearest to him. He nudged the carcass with his boot and inspected his kill. As he placed the barrel of the rifle against the bloodied coat and began to roll her over, the black cat hit him.

It hit him savagely, ripping his shoulder and clawing deeply into his face. Red Hawk screamed and fell back away from the cat. He tumbled down a steep grade. Falling, he lost his rifle. He didn't mind. The fall had taken him safely out of the black cougar's range. When he came to a stop he cursed himself for trying a head shot that had probably just stunned the little black bastard.

By the time he had regained his footing, one hand plastered to his bleeding face, the cat was gone.

Fiske's voice brought him back to reality. "What'd you say?"

"Nothing," muttered Red Hawk. "It's not important. Let's look at the corral."

He started to move ahead of them but Fiske tapped his shoulder with the end of his rifle barrel and he slowed up.

Solomon was trembling. Fiske was cautious, his mind partially diverted by the necessity of watching Red Hawk. His interest in the cougar was mostly curiosity. If it stayed on this range, it did not seem likely he would ever be required to mount a hunting posse to kill it to protect livestock. Few people lived in this section and fewer still kept livestock.

Still, it was his responsibility to check it out.

Solomon was scared. Of what, he did not know.

Red Hawk was furious. He kept running his hands over his face.

Each time his fingers brushed the outline of the scar his face got darker with anger.

"The same one," he muttered under his breath.

The three men moved around the shack and halted at the log railing. Red Hawk's mouth dropped open as he stared glassy-eyed, almost unbelieving. "Jesus!"

At the rear of the corral a large section of fencing had been completely destroyed. The heavy boards had been pulverized, pushed out from the inside by a massive blow. Pieces of splintered wood were everywhere. A bloody trail left the corral and cut through the meadow. It disappeared in the trees, heading directly up the side of Spirit House. The mare was in the same position she'd been in when Solomon had left for town.

Now the colt was gone.

5

There was a man, a thousand miles from Spirit House, beginning a journey, a journey that would bring him to Spirit House. The mountain called him as surely as it called Red Hawk.

The cream-colored sports car swung off the freeway, accelerated, hit the off ramp like a bullet and squealed to a stop at the bottom of the ramp.

John Skydancer smiled behind his black sunglasses.

The woman beside him lit a cigarette from the tip of her last one.

"I suppose it's the thought of seeing your ancestral home that gives you such a lead foot."

"Home? I always drive like hell is chasing me. It helps me relax."

She smiled, gave him a languorous sideways glance. "I thought that was what I was along for."

The car jerked forward, went right at Skydancer's touch and shot down a rutted dirt road, causing a cloud of dust to boil up behind them.

"You really were born on a reservation?" She stared at the bleak and desolate country they traveled through. "It doesn't quite go with your image."

"On a blanket, if you want to be accurate." Skydancer's head hit the ceiling as the car bottomed out in a deep rut. He eased up on the gas.

"I hate having to slow up here. This place depresses me. It's the kind of place you just want to drive through fast and try to forget."

"Some attitude to take toward your ancestral home," she said, mocking him. "John Skydancer, reservation-born corporation attorney for a strip-mining company. A million-a-year man who drives too fast, looks just a little too handsome for his own good and is about to seduce the boss's daughter."

She exhaled a puff of cigarette smoke. "If you ask me, it sounds like a bad movie."

He looked at her out of the corners of his eyes. "What do you mean, about to seduce the boss's daughter? *You* seduced me!"

"You can't count last night. I was drunk. Besides, nothing that happens in a Holiday Inn is real." She coughed once, from the dust leaking into the car from the open windows.

"You were sober. I thought *I* was the one who was drunk!"

"Typical Indian, one tiny bottle of vodka, half a bottle of champagne and a pitcher of martinis, and just like that, you're drunk. Typical man too. He can remember if he was drunk but not who seduced who."

"You're beautiful in the morning when you're hung over. The red veins in your eyes are sexy," he said, grimacing as the car hit another deep rut. He slowed up even more.

"You should talk. Even the lenses of your sunglasses are bloodshot."

The car hit another deep rut and they were thrown together.

"I'm getting a headache," she said. "For Christ's sake, slow down, the damn dust is pitting my complexion. Christ!" She choked as dust blew through the open window. "Are you sure somebody actually lives out here?"

"I grew up here. Lived here till I was eight or nine." Skydancer had to slow the car virtually to a crawl, as the road was almost obliterated by a wash. "When my father died, I was adopted by white folks in Phoenix. They moved back East and I did my teen years in upstate New York. My adoptive father went heavily into the stock market in the fifties, invested in something wild and crazy called Xerox in 1958 and hasn't had to do anything since except walk back and forth to the bank."

"That how you got into law school?"

"No. They let me in because I was so handsome. It's practically the only admission requirement Harvard Law School has."

She tossed her cigarette out the window. "The only thing worse than a good-looking guy is a guy who knows he's good-looking."

In contrast to Skydancer's dark skin, hair and eyes, she was as pale as a milk route. She had deep blue eyes and honey-blond hair from a bottle. She was thin and expensively dressed and beautiful if you read women's magazines and believed what you read.

She wore a layered look, part Salvation Army thrift bin and part Christian Dior.

No one seeing them together would ever say they were a couple.

An Indian in a three-piece suit still looks like an Indian.

A rich white woman dressed up as a Great White Hunter on methadone still looks like a rich white woman.

"Are you sure you really want to come out here with me?" he said, suddenly concerned. "I don't even know what it's going to be like, not after all these years, but it may not be too pleasant."

"If Daddy wants you to go a million miles out to the middle of nowhere and toss court injunctions at Indians, then I'm just stubborn enough to go too. Besides, it's our honeymoon. Besides, if you think I'm going to stay in that stupid Holiday Inn, you're crazy. Whither thou goest, so, uh . . . whatever. English lit. wasn't my subject."

"Did I mention that I love you."

He put his hand on her leg, giving it a squeeze.

"Not that I recall. I think mostly you just breathe heavy and your tongue hangs out. I'm not sure you can articulate."

He moved his hand abruptly, making her jump. She squealed.

"How's that for eloquence."

"You lawyers really know how to argue a case." She put her head on his shoulder.

The sun was blazing like a boiled lemon in the sky. The heat was oppressive, the dust heavy. Their collective hangovers made it worse. The road seemed to be endless.

"I think I see it," she said, looking through the windshield at something in the distance. "You must be excited. The homeland of your ancestors. The son of the people returns, to regain the lost ways, to ride the mighty buffalo sidesaddle, to be chief of his people once more, to . . ."

"There are times when you aren't even remotely funny. This is one of them." There was a hint of real anger in his voice.

"Who's trying to be funny? This is our honeymoon. Nothing is supposed to be funny on your honeymoon."

In the distance, a cluster of stone buildings lay sweltering in the heat. They were small, more the size of shacks than houses. Behind them, the black rim of a mesa towered. It was a desolate place, bleak and forbidding.

"Why exactly are we coming here? Ever since we started this idiot's quest, you've acted like the whole thing is some big mystery." There was a hint of gentle sarcasm in her voice. "Is it some kind of ceremonial reunion or something?"

"I don't have any close relatives here, if that's what you mean. It's just some legal business, routine stuff if you look at it a certain way, but it has to be done now. There's a deadline for filing, a very serious deadline and lots of money involved."

The car passed through a gate that sagged down toward the ground, once opened apparently, never closed since it was built. A few ghostly strands of wire was all that remained on each post of what once had been a barbed-wire fence.

Skydancer removed his sunglasses. A sheen of perspiration covered his forehead. "I'm probably going to feel as much a stranger here as you do."

"What kind of business does my father's company do out here? I can't believe there's anything out here worth anything. If this isn't the end of the world, it's at least within driving distance."

"A reservation is supposed to be land so bad nobody could think of any use for it, except to hide Indians on it. But they guessed wrong on this land. Uranium." Skydancer motioned with one hand toward the looming black mesa. "A lode of rich uranium ore right in the middle of Indian land. Your father's company has a permit to mine on Indian land. Permit notwithstanding, there's been a good deal of trouble about it."

"Let me guess. You're here to negotiate with the Indians because you're Indian, right? They won't talk to white lawyers but they'll talk to you."

He switched the car off. The buildings seemed deserted. No one came out to meet them.

"Something like that." He reached into the back seat for a briefcase."

"And you know all about being Indian because you went to Harvard."

"Especially because I went to Harvard." He smiled ironically.

She laughed and started to get out of the car. She regarded the silent buildings distrustfully. "I just hope you know what you're doing."

He stepped out of the car, stretching his cramped muscles. He stared at the decrepit buildings with a grim look on his face. He looked worried. "So do I."

6

Red Hawk stepped through the splintered rails where the cougar had taken the colt through the fence. He raised his fist and shook it at the mountain where the cat had gone.

"I'm gonna kill you, you black son of a bitch! YIIIIEEEEE!"

Red Hawk's cry of defiance echoed back distantly from the mountain.

"Gonna shout him to death?" asked Fiske sarcastically.

Solomon turned and began walking toward his cabin. He had discharged his debt to Spirit House, the mountain sacred to his people. He had brought Red Hawk back. As he walked away, he did not look back at his son.

"I'll spread the word around town about the cougar," said Sheriff Fiske, speaking to Solomon's departing back. Solomon kept on walking. He disappeared inside his cabin, pulling the heavy door closed with a slam.

Fiske turned around. Red Hawk met him halfway. One of the splintered corral rails crashed against the side of his head. He went down heavily on one knee.

He managed to hold on to his rifle even though Red Hawk had zeroed in on it and struggled to tear it from his grasp. Fiske kicked out, trying to knock Red Hawk's legs out from under him. He missed but Red Hawk slipped on the mare's blood and fell sideways across the dead horse.

Fiske staggered to his feet. Red Hawk, although handcuffed, was quicker. He got both hands under Fiske's gun barrel and swung upward with all the strength of his massive arms. The gun barrel whipped up, cracking Fiske across the face, the gunsight cutting deep into his forehead.

Fiske went over backward and Red Hawk dove on top of him. Again he struggled to wrest the gun away but stubbornly Fiske held on. Red Hawk couldn't get much leverage with his hands cuffed.

They rolled over and over in the blood and dust.

Red Hawk was twice Fiske's size and half his age. He should have taken him easily but Fiske was tougher than he looked, and was fighting for his life.

Fiske landed a solid punch to Red Hawk's jaw, catching him by surprise, pushing him back with the force of the blow. It gave him enough room to wedge the gun between them. Fiske rammed it against Red Hawk's chest and shoved.

The gun slammed under Red Hawk's chin. He fell backward off Fiske, gasping for air, clutching the underside of his throat.

Fiske shakily got to his feet. Using the gun as a club, he swung at Red Hawk's head.

The handcuffs saved Red Hawk. He tried to back up quickly, but lacking the counterbalance of his arms, he leaned back too far, falling. The stock of the rifle just grazed his head.

On the ground, he snatched up a fistful of dust and tossed it into Fiske's face. Fiske gagged, dust in his mouth and eyes. Blinded, he stumbled and went down, falling on top of the rifle.

Red Hawk looked around for a weapon, a board, anything. He seized the nearest thing to hand, the severed head of the mare.

He raised the gory head above his shoulders and smashed it down on the back of Fiske's head as he tried to rise.

The force of the blow slammed Fiske into the ground, face first. He lay where he fell, his head hanging at a strange angle.

Red Hawk wiped his bloody hand on his shirt, staggered forward until he stood over the still body of the sheriff. He dropped to his knees beside the body and shoved it over on its back.

Fiske seemed dead.

Red Hawk put his head against Fiske's chest. "Well, you ain't dead," said Red Hawk. "Not yet anyway, you bastard!"

He fumbled the handcuff keys out of Fiske's shirt pocket.

The cuffs opened and he tore them off savagely. His wrists were raw where the cuffs had abraded them. He yanked Fiske's legs together and fastened the cuffs to Fiske's ankles. He clinched them up tight enough to be really painful. He threw the keys back into the trees where no one would ever find them.

He got Fiske's rifle and laid it alongside the jeep. He came back for Fiske, put his hands under his armpits, dragged him to the jeep and slammed the unconscious body into the back seat. He removed the jeep's keys from the ignition and put them in his pocket.

That done, he tucked the rifle under his arm and sprinted to the cabin. He jerked on the door handle. The door was locked.

"Open up," he called out.

There was no sound from inside the cabin.

"Open this goddamn door!" he shouted. He banged on the door with the butt of the rifle.

"Go away. You are no longer welcome here," Solomon's voice answered.

"I don't give a good goddamn if I'm welcome or not, open this door, old man." Red Hawk slammed the butt of the rifle savagely into the door again. The door was solid and did not give. "All I want to do is get some of my stuff and get the hell out of here. I'm going up Spirit House after that black bastard cougar! Let me in, goddamnit!"

"You'll find all of your possessions on the other side of the house, in your car. You have nothing of yours in this house. You do not exist in this house."

Lianna's voice rang out suddenly from within. "Did you kill Sheriff Fiske?"

Red Hawk smashed the door again.

"He's alive," said Red Hawk. "But don't hold your breath. The day isn't over yet."

"Go away," said Lianna. "You are no son of mine."

Red Hawk slammed the door again.

"We put all your belongings in your car. Everything. All we ask is that you go away." Solomon's voice was calm.

Solomon stood on the other side of the door with a heavy rifle cradled in his arms.

Red Hawk gave the door a final kick in frustration and then went around to the back of the cabin. Inside, Lianna and Solomon heard his cry of rage as he discovered the burned-out hulk of his car with his burned clothes, guns and other possessions.

He came storming back around to the front.

"I'll kill you!" screamed Red Hawk, battering futilely at the door with the rifle butt.

"Go away or I'll shoot," said Solomon. He stood with his back straight, his old .30-30 trained on the door. He levered a shell calmly into the chamber.

Red Hawk turned the rifle around in his hands and fired into the hard wood of the door. The bullet passed just inches from Solomon's head. He did not flinch. He raised his gun and fired an answering shot.

Solomon's bullet passed so close to Red Hawk's head that it tore some of his hair away. He leapt back, frightened at the near-miss.

"You better save your bullets for the black cougar," said Solomon. "You will need them if you try to climb Spirit House."

Red Hawk shot into the door once more, then backed away and sprinted for the jeep.

The hell with them!

He'd get even with them later. After he'd killed the black cougar. Burn his car and all his stuff? Well, he'd show them. He'd come down off the mountain when they were asleep and fire the cabin. If they didn't get out in time, well, that would just be too damn bad. That would teach the bastards.

Same way he was going to teach that black cougar.

Solomon opened the door cautiously. Lianna said, "What are you going to do?"

Solomon levered another shell into his gun. "We can't let Red Hawk kill Sheriff Fiske. I will follow them and see that he doesn't come to harm."

"You would kill your own son to save a white man?" she asked.

"So it is, old woman, it is a crazy world. Mostly I shall watch and hope that I don't have to do anything."

"You can't kill Red Hawk. He belongs not to us but to Spirit House. Spirit House will be angry if you take him away from her."

"I wouldn't be killing my own flesh and blood. He does not exist in my heart anymore, but the call of the blood is ever strong. But I might shoot his leg once or twice, just to distract him, until I can get Sheriff Fiske safely away from him.

"But I shall not kill him. As much as I do not want it, the call of the blood is always there."

"Be careful, Solomon. I do not think Red Hawk feels the same call of the blood." Her face was bitter. "His heart is only a shadow and his blood is like poison from a night bush."

"He won't hear me and he won't see me. I will be like the shadow of a hawk. Seeing but not seen."

He went through the door and was gone.

Lianna waited until he was gone. Then she sat down in her old chair by the fireplace and began to weep softly for the son she had lost, for the son who now began a journey into the heart of Spirit House mountain.

7

The second traveler, also on a journey to the heart of Spirit House, pulled his briefcase out of the back seat of his sports car.

"Grab that other briefcase, will you," he said to his new wife, Pamela.

Pamela Skyler Tannerman Skydancer, an unblushing bride of exactly six days, grabbed the other briefcase obediently. She frowned at the unexpected weight as she lifted it by the handle.

"I've heard of two-fisted drinkers but two-briefcase lawyers! That's what I call ambitious!"

The briefcase banged heavily into her leg as she pulled it out of the car.

"Jesus! What you got in here, counselor? It weighs a ton!"

"It's the white man's burden," said Skydancer. "That's why you have to carry it."

"You're too funny for words. From now on, we communicate by spitting." The case started slipping out of her hands as she handed it to him. He lunged forward, seizing it in midair.

"Careful! Christ! If you had dropped that, our whole trip out here would have been wasted."

"What's in there? Hand grenades?"

"A Geiger counter. And a pretty delicate one at that."

He set the case carefully on the ground at his feet.

"Terrific! The big mystery of why we are here is explained! We're going to spend our honeymoon in the armpit of the world prospecting for uranium."

"It's not for anything as fun as all that, more's the pity. I'll tell you all about it later." His face darkened momentarily with dread and uncertainty. "That is, if I can figure out what there is to explain."

"I don't think I like mysteries," she said, coming to stand beside him as they looked at the desolate rows of reservation houses. The houses were small, stone-sided, of haphazard construction and in various states of disrepair. Several of them had collapsed walls and sagging roofs. It was a hot, desolate, uninviting place. "And I know I don't like this place," she said with a shudder. The poverty of the place was all too evident.

A door opened and two old men came slowly out into the hot sun. They were both quite old, similarly attired in high-crowned, black flat-brimmed hats, faded jeans and brightly colored Pendleton woolen shirts.

They walked slowly with the stiffened joints of their many winters. Their faces were like leather left too long in the desert sun. They came to a halt a few paces away, staring incuriously at the couple standing beside their shiny sports car.

"Hello," said Pamela, waving shyly at them.

She was nervous.

The old men just stared at them, not reacting.

John Skydancer felt the sweat oozing out on his forehead and on the backs of his hands.

He stepped up to them, put a hand out. "I'm John Skydancer. I represent Consolidated Uranium Mines, Tannerman, Inc."

His hand hung in the air like an unwelcome weed.

The old men looked at each other and shook their heads. They turned and walked back into the stone house, not saying a word, not looking back.

"What was that all about?"

"I don't know," said John Skydancer. "But it doesn't look good."

"What do we do now?" she asked, looking back at the car as if wishing they were back in it and heading elsewhere.

He was about to answer, but the doors of the houses nearest to them all opened, and as if a dam had burst, most of the people in the village came out in a wave. They walked slowly, women, children, men, young and old. They neither smiled in welcome nor frowned in disapproval. They just looked solemn.

"What do we do?" whispered Pamela, really scared.

"Smile," muttered Skydancer under his breath. He forced himself to smile, straightened his back and tried to project a calmness and self-assurance that he did not feel.

An old woman separated herself from the rest, came up and peered nearsightedly at Pamela.

"This one is white," she said. "She got bumps on her front end. A white girl, is my guess."

Pamela blushed.

The old woman moved past Pamela, and stood and peered closely into John Skydancer's face. She reached out and tugged on the lapel of his suit coat, forcing him to bend over a little down toward her.

She grabbed his cheeks with both hands and pinched.

He winced in surprise.

"This one is skin. Dressed white but skin, that's sure. You bet it's a damn funny way to come dressed . . ."

"I'm John Skydancer. I represent . . ." he started to interrupt.

"Shut up!" She waggled an accusatory finger in his face. "Don't be interrupting your elders."

"But . . ." he started to say.

She turned her back on him. "Come on. You must be thirsty."

She began walking through the people toward one of the stone houses. The others moved aside to let her through.

No one else spoke. They all just stood there silently.

"What do we do, John?" whispered Pamela.

"We get something to drink," Skydancer said, and began to follow the old woman.

Pamela walked so close to Skydancer's side they looked like Siamese twins as they passed through the silent crowd of Indians.

"Is this the way they welcome people they like or people they don't like?" she whispered.

He ducked so as not to hit his head on the top of a low doorway. "I don't know," he whispered back, holding tightly to his two briefcases. "But I think we're going to find out."

8

The jeep was parked at the end of a dirt road that overlooked a wide meadow. The open expanse of snow-whitened grass led to a range of low hills. Behind the hills, Spirit House mountain climbed toward the house of the sky.

Unseen, a figure moved like a shadow down toward the parked jeep.

Sheriff Fiske lay in the back seat. His eyes opened slowly. He did not try to move. He found it hard to believe that he was still alive. His ankles were handcuffed together.

Red Hawk pulled a heavy sheepskin-lined coat out of the back of the jeep. He slipped it on while Fiske turned his head, looking away from Red Hawk, looking up toward the distant peaks of Spirit House.

"You'll die up there," said Fiske. "I hope you do."

"Shut up."

Red Hawk had stopped at an old ranch house in the foothills before coming here. He'd been lucky. No one had been home. He'd stolen guns, ammo, food, clothes and other essentials. He emptied the jeep of the things he had taken.

Fiske nodded at the sun, just beginning to go down behind the tallest peak. "I'd wait till morning if I was you. This mountain is . . ."

Red Hawk pulled a .45 caliber automatic out of his belt, Fiske's own gun, and leveled it at Fiske's head. "Didn't you hear me? I said shut up!"

Sheriff Fiske shut up.

Red Hawk hefted a hunter's canvas backpack, settling it over his shoulder, cinching the straps across his chest.

He shaded his eyes, looking at the sun. "I've already wasted too much time. That cougar could be twenty miles in by now. A cat that big can travel fast when it knows somebody is after him."

"How's it supposed to know you're after it?" asked Fiske, forgetting that he was supposed to be quiet.

"If it doesn't, it will soon enough." Red Hawk turned, ready to leave, staring coldly at Fiske, his hand tightening on the handle of the .45.

Fiske saw the look and understood. "Might as well. One more murder isn't going to matter."

Red Hawk smiled. "Yeah. They can't electrocute me twice, can they?"

He lifted the gun.

Solomon Hawk moved among the trees, edging down closer to his son. He rested his rifle on the fork of a tree, steadying the sights so that they were fixed on his son, Red Hawk.

He pulled the hammer back, cocking the weapon as Red Hawk raised his gun.

The right leg, thought Solomon, that would be best. Hopefully, that would be enough. His hands were shaking and his eyes seemed aswim with tears but the old man knew he would not miss. The bullet should strike just above Red Hawk's right knee.

"Waste of bullets, though," said Fiske, trying to appear calm, although it was his own life he was bargaining for. "I'm not going up there after you. Nobody else is either. It would take an army to ferret you out up there. Even then they might not find you. If you make it up there, if the mountain doesn't kill you or that cougar or the cold or any of the hundred other ways you could die up there, you're home free. You get up there, the law will be the least of your worries."

"You could tell them where I went up," said Red Hawk, closing his hand over the pistol grip.

"I could," said Fiske, feeling sweat breaking through on his face and back. "I will, but will it do them any good?"

Red Hawk appeared indecisive. His finger found the trigger, then released it. He lowered the gun a little bit, trying to make up his mind. He looked away, looked back up toward Spirit House mountain.

Solomon narrowed his eyes, tightened his grip on the rifle and began to pull gently on the trigger, an even, slow pressure.

Red Hawk turned away.

"The hell with it."

He shoved the gun into the waistband of his pants. Killing Fiske just wasn't fun enough to justify it.

Solomon shuddered, his muscles straining as he let go of the trigger, and brought the shot back from that tiny moment of being or not being. It had been very close. His muscles spasmed from the strain and the rifle would have fallen from his nerveless hands if the tree branch had not supported its weight.

Red Hawk tossed the jeep keys into a snowdrift beside the jeep. "I'd shoot you, Fiske, but the cougar might be close and I don't want to spook him."

Fiske sighed with relief.

"You're going to look funny as hell trying to drive down these mountain roads with your ankles handcuffed together," said Red Hawk.

He turned his back on Fiske and began moving across the meadow toward the slopes of Spirit House.

Fiske reached down under the seat, going for the .38 concealed under the front passenger seat. His hands closed on the barrel and he pulled it out. He turned it in his hand, aiming for the center of Red Hawk's back.

At this distance, he couldn't miss. His finger squeezed the trigger. The hammer clicked. The gun did not fire.

Red Hawk heard the metallic click and turned and looked back at Fiske. The sheriff still had the gun pointed at him. Fiske pulled the trigger again.

Click.

Nothing happened.

Red Hawk had something clasped tightly in the palm of his left hand. He swung his arm back and tossed it at Fiske, showering .38 cartridges over the jeep.

"Works better if you put bullets in it." Red Hawk laughed. Turning his back on Fiske, he moved on across the meadow.

Fiske caught one of the shells against his chest. He had time to reload, maybe get a shot off, but he didn't bother. He knew when he was outclassed. At least now he could shoot the handcuffs open and drive back down the mountain safely.

Solomon threw his gun in the snow. He watched the one who had been his son go off toward Spirit House. He no longer had a son. Red Hawk belonged to Spirit House now, to whatever justice, to whatever death awaited him there.

Solomon wanted to turn around, to walk away, to go as silently as he had come.

But the feelings of a father for a son are not so easily forgotten.

With an aching heart, he watched Red Hawk as he moved up the slope, seeing him for the last time. He knew he would stand there and watch until Red Hawk was out of sight.

Fiske too watched Red Hawk as he moved into the cover of the trees, disappearing finally from sight. I'm damn lucky to be alive, he thought, damn lucky.

Another pair of eyes watched Red Hawk too.

From a ledge high on the mountainside, the black cougar sat astraddle the dead body of the colt. The colt's head had been bitten off cleanly. The meat had gone untouched, for, strangely, the cougar did not eat what it killed.

As Red Hawk passed through the trees, the cougar's jaws caught up the bloody head of the colt.

With a snarl, it began moving down the mountain, down toward Red Hawk.

As Red Hawk began his journey to Spirit House, the heart of the mountain began to stalk him.

In a place far away, it began to stalk yet another man.

9

The old woman ushered them into a small stone-sided house. An old man sat in the center of the room on a bright-hued Indian blanket of Zuni design. The old woman gave them each a gourd of water.

John looked around inside the room, looking in vain for chairs.

Pamela caught on quicker. She moved forward and sat on the edge of the rug, near the old man. She sipped her water in silence, staring at the old man. The old man stared back.

He was dressed like a ranch hand, faded jeans, long hair braided on one side, scuffed cowboy boots and Pendleton shirt.

John Skydancer set his briefcases down on the floor and stood uncomfortably beside Pamela.

"Are you Black Two Bears?" asked John uncertainly.

The old woman went out the door without so much as a word or glance in their direction.

The old man did not speak.

The silence in the room was almost unbearable.

The room itself was almost bare of furniture. Two cots along one wall covered with Indian blankets. An old stove that burned wood stood in one corner. The stovepipe was connected to a hole in the ceiling. A table with a bucket of water and a bundle of wood stood in the other corner.

There was an air of poverty and hardship in the room.

"Excuse me, are you Black Two Bears or could you direct me to Black Two Bears?" began Skydancer again.

"I'm him," said the old man calmly. He looked up at Skydancer. "Sit down. I get pain in the neck looking up at you."

"Fine," said Skydancer. He sat down awkwardly next to Pamela.

"Wife?" asked the old man.

Skydancer nodded.

"Nice-looking woman. Strong legs. Should have lots of children. Bet she spit them out like piñon nuts," said the old man.

The old man took an old corncob pipe out of his shirt pocket and began chewing on the stem.

"Well, I'm . . ." Skydancer began, as he realized that this was not going to go easily at all.

Pamela interrupted. "Thank you."

"So," said the old man, and then he stopped talking.

Skydancer licked his lips nervously. "What I have come to discuss is the signing of . . ." He had opened his briefcase and removed a sheaf of legal documents.

"Oh yes," said the old man. "You got any tobacco?"

"Cigarettes," said Skydancer, thrown off stride again. "I've just got cigarettes."

The old man shook his head no.

Skydancer began again. "These papers indemnify Consolidated Uranium Mines, Tannerman, Inc., from any damages related to . . ."

"And pay money too, right?" said the old man with a grin. "Money make everything right, ain't that so?"

Skydancer almost stuttered. "Uh, well, uh, yes. There *is* a considerable compensation for . . ."

The old man waved his hand, motioning for him to be quiet.

"Are you an honest man? Do you walk in life with a good heart?" asked the old man. "Everything else, what does it matter?"

Skydancer shrugged. "I suppose I am as honest as the next man."

"Which next man is that?" wondered the old man. "Well, never mind. Let me talk to you, young man. You are Indian even though you are dressed up all white and have a pretty white wife. I was troubled in my heart and I said to your company, there are answers I must have. I said, send me a man who can ease the trouble in my heart and in the hearts of my people."

"I intend to make all the difficulties engendered in the . . ."

"Do not interrupt me. I talk plain and do not understand it much when you yourself do not talk plain."

The old man waved his corncob pipe for emphasis.

"We moved out village because the white men say there is harmful invisible things that will make our children sick. All this because of the strange things that are dug out of the ground. We were promised many things in return for this. We did not want to move, for we had lived there for many, many winters and it was our home. But we had no choice. That is what we were told."

Skydancer stirred uncomfortably on the floor.

"We were given money, which melted like snow and bought nothing. When it came time to build new house, we got no help from your company until much noise and shouting was begun. Then the company came and they built us these houses out of stone which had been cut from the ground beside the mine.

"Now the white man doctors say the stone is contaminated. It causes the invisible sickness, yet we live in these houses as we have been told to do. We asked the company to come and explain what is going on but they tell us in such a way that we do not understand."

"It is my job to make you understand. That's why I'm here," said Skydancer.

"Some of the children are sick. They throw up their food and have sores on their skin. We wish to know why this is so."

Skydancer reached for his other briefcase, pulling it next to him. He opened it and took out the Geiger counter.

"I've brought this. It is a machine that will tell if the buildings you live in are safe."

"I do not trust the white man's machines much," said the old man.

"Believe me. With this machine, I can prove that there is no latent or harmful radioactive material within the housing structures our company has constructed."

Pamela looked at Skydancer. Skydancer was nervous, his face covered in sweat. She knew he was lying, or at least suspected it.

"I don't understand what you say. I wish only for our children to be safe. I want them to be healthy and strong and to live a good life. Can your machine promise that?"

"Yes. You have my word on it."

"Is your word good?"

"It's better than a white man's word," said Skydancer. "If that counts for anything."

"I don't know," said the old man. There was fear in his eyes. "So many have lied to us. It is hard to know who to trust."

"If John Skydancer were not a trustworthy man, I would not have married him," said Pamela.

The old man smiled. "It is always good to have the heart of a woman believing in you."

Pamela smiled at the old man in return.

Skydancer stood up and went to one of the walls of the room. He unfolded the Geiger counter probe and aimed it at the wall.

The old man watched him curiously.

The machine began to click faintly as John turned it on. He fiddled with the volume knob. He went up and down the length of the wall with the probe. The machine made only a faint click.

"It is a Geiger machine. I have seen the engineering men use it before," said the old man. "It measures the invisible things."

Skydancer hesitated at the wall. There was a very strange look on his face.

Skydancer then pointed the probe at the face of his watch. The Geiger counter made a loud and rapid clicking noise. John Skydancer tried to smile but something was bothering him.

Pamela gasped, sensing something wrong, something very wrong.

"If the stone walls of this house were contaminated, it would make a loud noise, many, many clicks in a very rapid beat. There is radiation in everything," said Skydancer. "By hearing only a very faint clicking noise, I have just proved that the walls are . . ." He looked back at the wall guiltily. "Safe. They have even less radiation than a . . . than a watch. So you see, there is no danger to you or to your children. There was some other reason why the children were sick."

"I myself thought it might be from eating the bad food of the white people, but I do not know," said the old man gravely. The old man looked worried. "This is a true thing, what you have said?"

Skydancer licked his lips nervously.

"It is true and not a white man's clever lie or running away from the truth?" The old man's voice trembled.

Skydancer could not meet the old man's eyes.

Pamela spoke for him. "John Skydancer is the most honest man I know. If he says it is true, then it is true. John loves children. We plan on having some of our own, as soon as we can. He'd never do anything to hurt children."

Skydancer looked at her sharply in surprise, for Pamela had expressed a very definite disinterest in ever having children. In fact, she'd said she hated children. The lies seemed to come more easily to her lips than to his own.

"He loves children as much as I do. He's too Indian to lie to you. Don't let the suit and my presence fool you. He may have married a white woman, but his sympathies have always been with the Indians."

The old man looked first at her and then at Skydancer. There was doubt and fear intermingled on his face. His responsibilities for his people's future weighed heavily on him.

"My heart wants to believe," he said, "but my stomach is scared."

The old man looked at John Skydancer.

Skydancer forced himself to meet his stare. His own future rode on it.

"I have told the truth."

"Then why is it that the company is offering us money if we will sign these papers? That is what I do not understand."

John Skydancer stretched his hands out, as if encompassing the entire reservation. "It is the wish of upper management," he began, then stopped, for that was not the right approach.

"It is only to make up for the trouble moving to a new place has caused. It is to show your people that our company is grateful for the cooperation your people have shown us. And also, it is because your people are poor. They live in poverty and it is the wish of the company that poverty be ended for you."

The old man put down his pipe. "There was a great rock found in the Third World by the Hero Twins. The Twins attacked it, chipping it away. This rock was Poverty. They chipped away until Poverty was almost destroyed. Then Poverty said to the Twins, 'Please do not destroy me, for when I am gone, what will you have left to fight?' The Hero Twins of old let Poverty survive, which is why it lives in this world today."

Pamela had an answer for that. "With money, one can buy better food for the children, warmer clothes. The best medical care so that they can grow strong and healthy. You can't turn your back on this money. For their sakes. If money can make life better for your children, perhaps they will not have the sicknesses that they now suffer."

"It may be so," said the old man. "I often worry it is the bad white man's food that they eat."

"Will you sign these papers? Will the other members of the tribal council also sign? Without these papers, the mining cannot go on, your people will not be taken care of and we will not be able to help your people," said Skydancer, and as he said it he began to hate himself.

"If I sign, they will all sign."

Pamela took the paper from Skydancer and handed it to the old man. John Skydancer moved as if to take it back and then stopped. Pamela stared at him, just for a second, coldly, almost calculatingly, and he restrained himself.

Pamela took a ballpoint pen from Skydancer's coat pocket and held it out to the old man.

"You are a good-hearted woman," said the old man. "A man who has a good-hearted woman has a good life."

Skydancer could not look at Pamela.

"Where do I sign?"

John Skydancer wanted to show him but guilt made him paralyzed. Pamela opened the papers and competently made X's on the lines where Black Two Bears must sign.

She gave her husband a look which said, "Don't blow it, John."

"I must do this for the good of my people's children. But I hope it is the right thing because I only wish to do the right thing," said the old man solemnly.

Skydancer made his face a blank, unreadable mask.

"You won't regret this," said Pamela to the old man as he signed "Black Two Bears."

John Skydancer felt a cold knife of ice in his heart, because he knew the old man would regret it.

10

The drive back to town was made in silence. Skydancer grimly threaded his way back through the back roads and treacherous potholes.

When they were just a few miles out of town, Pamela spoke.

"You didn't even tell them which tribe you belonged to. You missed out on the ceremonial homecoming."

"I was too ashamed."

"Of me? Of your white wife?"

He turned and looked at her. "No. Of me."

"I thought it all went very well. I'm sure my father will be very pleased."

"You knew what this trip was all about from the very beginning, didn't you?" said Skydancer suddenly.

"Let me just say that it was discussed."

"By whom? When?"

Skydancer braked to a sudden stop. Pamela looked uncomfortable.

"John, it's hot out here. Couldn't we talk this out back at the goddamn hotel?"

Skydancer got out of the car and came around to her side. He opened the door for her. "No. I want to talk about it now."

She got out of the car and stood in front of him.

"By whom?"

"My father of course."

"Why?"

She looked irritated. "Oh, grow up, John. It's over and done with. The papers are signed. My father is assured of your worth to the company and the two of us can look forward to . . ."

"What the hell are you talking about?" He was angry and confused.

"Look, John. My father told you you had to put across this deal, didn't he? If you wanted to make it in the company, it was crucial that you put across the deal before the deadline. He told you all this before we left, didn't he?"

"Yes," said John. "He told me all that."

"I believed in you, John. I knew you'd come through. My father had doubts but I want you to know that I believed in you."

"It was a test, right? A goddamn test!" Skydancer was furious.

Pamela was calm. She knew how to handle him.

"He doesn't know we're married, John. Until you get back with those papers, we don't even have his permission to marry. It was the last and only condition he made. I lied to you, John. I admit it. I said we had his permission to go off and get married. But he doesn't know."

Skydancer was angry down to the bone. "His goddamn permission! Not good enough to marry his goddamn . . . You set me up. You and your father both."

"Shut up, John! I married you because I knew you'd come through. You're like me, John. You do what has to be done, no matter what the cost."

Pamela turned away from him, opened the door and got back into the car.

"That Geiger counter was rigged," said John. "They told me how to do it. They told me what to say and how to use it. I played my part like an actor and all the time I was doing it I knew that stone wall was . . ."

"Deadly, John. Full of radiation," finished Pamela. "In a few years or so, it'll cause a lot of trouble, but we will have had another few years of trouble-free mining because we got them to sign."

"What if I tear this paper up?" said Skydancer. "What if I tear the goddamn paper to shreds!"

She reached into her purse and took out another paper. It was a marriage license. "Then you might as well tear this one up too, John."

Skydancer got back into the car. He sat there for a few seconds, saying nothing, feeling nothing. Then he started the car and drove on.

The marriage license was back in her purse.

The contract was back in his briefcase.

And John Skydancer was now on a cold journey to the heart of Spirit House.

11

Red Hawk held his breath, bringing the cross hairs of the scope up, centering them on the black cougar. The long dark shadow crouched on a ridge a hundred yards up the slope, silhouetted by the burning moon.

Red Hawk expelled his breath, waiting a two count, then squeezed the trigger.

The thunderous report of the shot crashed back from the mountain.

A puff of dirt kicked up just short of the standing cat. Red Hawk grimly reslung the rifle and started up the mountain again. He couldn't understand how he had missed.

The cat raised its head, watching Red Hawk climb. It stood over something that lay at its feet. It did not stir from the ridge. It seemed almost to be waiting for Red Hawk.

Farther up the slope, Red Hawk halted, again gauging the distance. He sighted in on the cougar. The cat loomed large in the sight. This time he could not miss. The wind picked up, making the gun barrel waver. He took his eyes from the scope to fasten the rifle sling around his elbow to steady his aim.

When he looked back into the scope, the ridge was barren of life.

12

Skydancer had to take a two-day vacation from his honeymoon to file the papers before the deadline.

The 727 sat on the terminal apron, its engines revving up. The ground crew unhooked fuel lines, checked panels. A man in white coveralls lifted John Skydancer's suitcase, turned with it and dropped it roughly onto the moving belt. The suitcase wobbled forward with the other bags to the loading bay of the plane.

At a window in first class, John Skydancer peered out, not really looking at anything. He held his overcoat firmly in his lap as if it were a shield he was carrying into battle.

In the empty seat next to him rested his briefcase. The contract lay inside like an unexploded grenade.

In the aisle seat next to him a white-haired man in a business suit was doing a crossword puzzle. In front of the man was a bulkhead that separated the passenger compartment from the flight deck.

A young stewardess busied herself with the automatic coffee machine in the bulkhead galley. She had the face of a much-vexed nanny.

As she bent over to check the coffeepots resting in inset depressions in the bulkhead, her skirt hiked up.

The businessman whistled appreciatively.

Surprised, the stewardess lost her balance and dropped a coffeepot that was only halfway back into the recess. The coffeepot slammed into the receptacle but did not mesh with the restraining bracket meant to hold it in flight.

The girl recovered her poise, glared at the man who had whistled, then walked back quickly to the rear of the plane.

Skydancer paid no attention.

A hairline crack appeared in the coffeepot.

The aircraft began moving down the runway. Skydancer stared indifferently at the buildings and sheds going by, holding his coat tighter as the sounds of the engine built to a tremendous roar.

The plane rose without incident into the night and leveled off. The *thump* that accompanied the closing of the rear bay doors caused Skydancer to grip his armrest, his fingernails digging into the fabric.

It also caused the unsecured coffeepot to smash against the restraining bracket. Coffee began leaking down into the heating element.

The plane rose at a steep angle, climbing quickly to breast the mountains in its path. There were clouds in the mountains ahead and a storm was brewing on Spirit House mountain, whose peaks reached up toward the oncoming plane.

Skydancer watched the night sky and thought of the night before, the fight he and Pamela had had while he packed.

His wife was sitting on the edge of the hotel-room bed, watching him throw his clothing into the suitcase. She held a glass of scotch in her hand.

"Are you sure you can manage it all by yourself?" she said, her voice slurred with whiskey. "Or should I go along to wipe your nose."

Skydancer didn't say anything.

"It's really very simple. You hand Father the papers, properly filed before the deadline. He gives you a cigar, says welcome to the family, and you come dashing back to marry the girl you've already married."

"Just like that. It sounds so easy when I hear you tell it."

"I was thinking we could finish our honeymoon in Las Vegas."

"Perfect!" said Skydancer. "A real goddamn appropriate choice."

"Christ! You don't like anything, do you? You've been cranked off ever since we got back! When are you going to get over this crap?"

He tossed a shirt into the suitcase and then slammed the lid down savagely.

"Maybe never."

"Look, John." Pamela spilled some of her drink on the bed-spread. "Let's cut out the crap. When you married me, you made a commitment. You can't throw away your education or our chance at a decent future just because of some goddamn misguided loyalty to people you don't even really know. You're not Indian anymore, John. You're white. You've been educated out of it."

"Maybe."

"You don't owe them anything."

"Do you know what I'm doing to them? Do you have any idea what kind of . . ." He couldn't finish the sentence. His shoulders slumped and he seemed tired, as if he had walked a hundred miles for each year of his life.

"I'm taking you to the airport, John. You can say anything you want to say, do anything you want to do. You make the choice, you make the decision. You can go back and turn your briefcase in for a bow and arrow if you want to." She downed the rest of her drink and tossed the empty glass aside. "But I won't be waiting here for you if you do."

He tried to put his arms around her but she pushed him away. She pushed his briefcase between them and shoved it into his stomach.

"Do something with it, John. Then we'll think about what we'll do with each other."

Skydancer said, "I didn't know it was like that."

They didn't even kiss at the airport.

It was like that.

13

"A drink might help," said the man in the aisle seat.

"What?" said Skydancer, startled, turning away from the window, from the dimly lit mountains passing beneath the plane.

"Press that button up there. One of those half-clad young chicks will bring you anything you want." The man smiled at Skydancer's apparent confusion. "This your first time in an airplane?"

"What? . . . No. Uh, I fly all the time."

"Sure you do." The man leaned over the unoccupied seat between them and smiled. "None of my business, young man, but you hold my coat any tighter, it's gonna be a vest."

Skydancer looked down at the man's topcoat in his lap. His fingers had compressed it into a tight ball. He winced and hastily unfolded it.

"Sorry. Had my mind on something else," he said, handing the man back his coat.

"Hell, no need to apologize." The man paused as he stared at Skydancer. "Woman trouble, huh?"

Skydancer managed a weak smile. "Is there any other kind?"

The hairline crack in the coffeepot widened. Coffee seeped through as the motion of the aircraft sloshed it back and forth. It filled up the recess under the coils of the heating element and began leaking down on the wires that connected to the heating element.

Skydancer put his head back against the seat. He had ordered three drinks and downed them all quickly. He was tired and tried to sleep. He dozed fitfully.

A dream tugged at the edges of his consciousness.

He seemed to be falling. A dark mountain loomed up.

Skydancer was an arrow, plunging down toward the stone face of a mountain.

But the dream twisted like a snake, changing its skin in a fever. Now Skydancer was driving his car up the side of a mountain. The engine was a Geiger counter, and when he stepped on the gas, the Geiger counter clicked like an angry rattlesnake.

He was being pursued by children, mad children, hairless, with ugly sores on their faces and hands. They pursued him through the night, trying to catch him, drag him down with them, cover him in blackness and death. But he had his car and he drove fast.

He was speeding up the side of a big mountain, and every time it seemed they were almost on him, his car found a new road, always going higher.

He would be safe on the mountain.

Up there on top of the world, where no one could touch him. It was a terrifying dream.

At the last moment, he thought he broke away, that he left the whole world behind, as his car roared clicking up the last road to the top of the mountain, but the car plunged up and over and fell into nothingness and he was falling down the mountain, falling, falling, falling.

The dream was shattered by the crackling of the intercom.

"Ladies and gentlemen, we are approaching some fairly heavy turbulence at this altitude. We've asked for a course correction to try to get under the turbulence and it has been approved, so we'll be dropping down a few thousand feet and we'd appreciate it if you'd all buckle your seat belts and remain seated until we make the course correction. Thank you."

The captain's voice died in the hum of conversation in the crowded cabin. The aircraft yawed five degrees. The crack in the coffeepot broadened. Coffee flowed down through the metal partition separating galley from flight deck, pooling behind the bulkhead.

On the other side of the bulkhead, directly below the spreading pool of coffee, was a circuit board. The mass of wires and connectors shared the space with oxygen lines that fed fore and aft. Green plastic tubing coiled around the board, leading to recesses holding the main oxygen storage bottles belowdecks.

The plane bumped through an air pocket. The coffee dropped on the circuit board. A small wisp of smoke rose from the bank of switches, then a spark as two wires arced under a loop of oxygen hosing.

The coffee continued to drip on the board.

The damage spread.

14

Red Hawk sat in front of a small campfire. The night air on the mountain was bitterly cold. He pulled a blanket around his shoulders as he chewed on a strip of beef jerky. Three times he had had the big black cougar in his sights only to have the cat leap away at the last minute. Farther and farther he had been led into the farthest reaches of Spirit House, the cougar always one jump ahead of him.

His rifle stood propped against a rock beside him, within easy reach. In his lap, he cradled a .45 automatic.

The ground around the fire was crisscrossed with patches of snow. He shivered. He dropped another pile of twigs on the fire and fire shadows danced on dark trees around him.

He stared into the gloom, trying to pierce the shadows.

"I know you're out there," he said. He touched the scar on his face, the old wound that was his souvenir from his first meeting with the black cougar long ago. "Can you feel it, black one? I've got your heart in my hands. I'm going to kill you."

Under the trees the brush moved and the sound of heavy breathing carried across the snow. Something stalked beyond the light of the fire.

Behind the sitting man a giant head rose and pushed through the foliage. The cat lowered its belly to the ground and crept silently to the edge of the firelight.

Red Hawk's back was to the cat as he reached to throw another branch on the fire. As his hand closed on the stick, he stiffened. His spine tingled, as if singed with a live wire. His hand moved back from the twig and inched slowly toward the rifle. He almost had his fingers on the gun.

His other hand moved, hidden from the cat's view by his body. Without really seeing it, he knew the sound was the big black cougar.

He reversed the position of the gun in his lap, thumbing the safety catch on the .45 to the off position.

The metallic click of the released safety was soft but the cougar heard it.

Screaming like a whirlwind from the house of hell, the cougar sprang.

Red Hawk heard the crashing of brush behind him and dove forward into the campfire. Spinning, he brought the pistol up, firing as he rolled over the blazing coals. The three-foot lance of flame from the muzzle split the air just under the hurtling cougar.

Red Hawk spun to the left as the cat landed on the other side of the fire.

Red Hawk stumbled to his feet, his blanket ablaze. He got off another quick shot. The slug went wild, breaking the branches overhead.

He stumbled forward toward the fire, heaving the burning blanket from him. The cat moved.

Red Hawk stood almost in the fire, blinded by the light and smoke. Leveling his pistol, he emptied the clip into the shadows at the far side of the fire.

With the fading of the last blast the clearing was plunged into silence.

Red Hawk squinted through the haze. The ground around the fire was bare save for churned white snow. There was no body, no blood on the snow.

Red Hawk had not even come close.

The black cougar was gone.

The spark on the circuit board became a small glow. There was not much oxygen in the bulkhead, so it flickered and almost died. Another circuit arced and a tiny draft fanned it into life. It brightened and licked at the oxygen lines above it. The plastic smoldered, then began to melt.

On the other side of the bulkhead, three uniformed flight officers rested in high-backed chairs, calmly carrying out their flight procedures. None of them noticed the smoke.

A trouble light flashed on and then off, as the circuit which controlled it fused out. No one noticed it the few seconds it was lit.

The airplane had reached the foothills of Spirit House mountain.

Red Hawk pushed on, the dark falling all around him. Red Hawk cursed himself for a fool. He should never have left the fire. It was that damn cougar. It was almost like it was leading him, tempting him to come and get him.

It was maddening.

A huge boulder divided the trail in front of him.

He studied it, decided it was too big to go over, then headed to the left, the only likely-looking way to go around. At least the trail was fairly level here.

Just as he rounded the boulder, the cougar screamed. It was so close Red Hawk jumped. The cougar had to be just on the other side of the rock.

He dropped his pack to allow more freedom of movement. He levered a shell into the chamber of his rifle. He edged warily around the side of the rock.

Almost around the corner, he steadied his rifle, jumped out, ready to fire.

The clearing on the other side of the boulder was empty. The cougar screamed.

Too late, he looked up.

The black cougar launched itself from the rock above him. It looked like a black fiend from the house of hell as it fell on him.

Red Hawk tried to lift his rifle but the cat slammed him into the ground. Red Hawk's head smashed into a rock as he went down, knocking him out cold.

Before he lost consciousness, in that brief instant before the black one hit him, Red Hawk had time for only one thought.

I'M DEAD.

Hours passed. A storm lashed the lower slopes of Spirit House, buffeting a large 727 thundering through the cold dark night. But here, for a time, the sky was clear, the storm not yet reaching high enough to touch this place. The moon rose in the sky, bathing the still figure in the moonlight.

The body of Red Hawk gleamed redly in the moonlight.

15

"You guys can ride me all you want," Brandon, the copilot, said. "But I tell you, marrying her was the best thing that ever happened to me."

"Cleared up your face finally, did it?" said the flight engineer, and he broke up in laughter. The pilot seemed not to hear the joke. He studied the instrument panels in front of him, looking worried.

"She's got this little five-year-old named Chrissie. Just like a little angel. I'm telling you, I never been around kids before, didn't think I ever wanted to be, but I really go for this little kid."

The flight engineer sighed in mock despair. "Just think of all those stewardesses you're going to miss. Brandon, you went and ruined yourself."

"I'm even thinking of giving up flying," said Brandon. "I think I've had all the thrills I need. I'd like to settle down, spend more time with them if I could."

The flight engineer was shocked. He turned to the pilot. "Are you listening to this guy?"

The pilot turned with a strange look on his face. "Something's wrong."

The look on the pilot's face stopped the flight engineer cold.

"You smell smoke?" asked the pilot, his face white and tense. "I think I've got an electrical short. My safeties don't read and the trouble light indicators are dead."

The lights in the cockpit flickered.

"Can you locate the short, Brandon?" said the pilot to the copilot. "Is it confined within the cockpit?"

Brandon frantically opened one of the circuit board panels, his face deathly white.

"I'm losing instrument control. The automatics are going," said the pilot, reaching for the radio, every inch a professional. "I'm going to SOS our . . ."

Suddenly the instrument board flashed as the oxygen line broke. Flame shot down the metal partition. The space between the flight deck and the galley was instantly ablaze.

"Radio's dead," said the pilot, outwardly calm. He turned and looked at Brandon and the flight engineer. "Intercom is dead too. Can't even tell the passengers how . . ."

Smoke leaked into the cockpit.

"Well, it looks like we're going to buy a piece of that farm in the sky," said the pilot.

"OH MY GOD! JULIE! CHRISSIE!" screamed Brandon. "This can't happen now! I love . . ."

The oxygen bottles blew. The glass in the cockpit exploded outward.

The pilot made a desperate lunge for his mask. He had it almost to his face when a lance of flame shot out from the mask, scorching his face and lungs. The other two men instinctively tried to rise, but there was no place to go.

A ball of fire engulfed the cockpit.

They were dead before they were sucked out the blown ports into the cold night sky.

The air at thirty thousand feet was thin, almost nonexistent. The flames poured out of the flight deck, raking back along the fuselage. Then the flames retraced their path and went out. They had exhausted the available oxygen. The emptied oxygen containers were burnt-out shells.

The 727 nosed down twenty-five degrees.

A stewardess in the rear of the plane tried vainly to balance a tray she held. Grabbing at the nearest seat back, she lost it, spilling drinks and mixed nuts on the head of a Catholic priest. The stewardess hit the deck as the aircraft dipped another ten degrees.

A man across the aisle from the Catholic priest tried to stand up.

He stepped on the stewardess's wrist, fracturing it. She screamed and let go of the seat leg she was holding. Her fingers scraped against the carpet as she slid down the aisle through the screaming passengers. She came to a violent halt against the flight-deck door, her neck broken, her sightless eyes staring at the overhead lights.

The lights dimmed, then went out. Pandemonium reigned. High-pitched wails filled the cabin as the ports blew. Weak calls for help came from throats too contorted from oxygen starvation to scream for help.

The oxygen masks failed to descend. It would have made little difference. There was no longer any contained oxygen aboard the aircraft.

The man next to Skydancer struggled to rise, reaching frantically for the overhead panel where the useless masks rested. Skydancer watched him as if in a dream. Skydancer was strapped firmly in his seat and the tilt of the plane caused him to extend his arms and brace himself on the seat back in front of him.

As the other man tugged at the overhead door the plane banked sharply to the right. The panel opened and the man caught the mask, trying to use it to steady himself. The tubing broke and he fell away from Skydancer, his hand reaching out for help.

Skydancer could only stare at him. He opened his mouth but no words came out. The man held on to the outside armrest, his body angling away. He reached for Skydancer, an expression of horror on his face. Skydancer looked at the outstretched hand, wanting to reach out, but his muscles refused to obey. His oxygen-starved body was rigid with fear.

Then the man was crushed against the ceiling as the plane went over.

Red Hawk stirred, slowly moved his hands. His head throbbed. His shoulders were pressed against sharp rocks. A huge weight seemed to be crushing his chest. His eyes opened, his lips moved. I'm still alive, he thought, dazed, not understanding.

One hand closed on the butt of his rifle. He was dizzy. He couldn't remember what had happened. Something rested heavily on his chest. He tried to raise himself, tried to sit up.

The bloody thing fell against his legs. Red Hawk shoved it away with one hand, trying to get it off his body. Now he remembered. The black cougar. His hand came away from the object across his legs covered with blood.

Red Hawk touched his chest. Blood. He was soaked in blood.

The moon made the mountain almost as bright as day. His hand turned the thing on his legs. He realized then what it was. And screamed, flinging it off him.

The black cougar had given him a gift.

The head of a colt.

16

The cat topped a rise and stopped, looking toward the sky. Its ears tilted forward at the sound of jet engines. The screech of the falling aircraft grew loud over the breathing of the cat.

A loud explosion in the distance turned the ridge to daylight. The cat bellied low to the ground, its fur rising on its back. The light faded and the cat rose. Not the least bit frightened, the cougar moved on, taking long easy strides over the rough ground.

On the mountainside Red Hawk slept fitfully in a cave. At the narrow entrance a fire burned brightly. He was wrapped in the remains of his scorched blanket. He kept his rifle cocked and ready in his hands. The sound of the second explosion shook the peaks. Red Hawk stirred in his sleep, clutching the rifle tighter. Even in sleep his face was tight with fear.

Dawn came to the mountain. Tiny rivulets of pure water ran through boulders, searching for creek beds that had been buried all winter.

A brightly plumed bird pivoted in the sky, looking for its breakfast. It flew down to the ground.

Skydancer was still strapped in, in what was left of his seat. Only the top of his head extended from the snowbank that imprisoned his body. He was in a tunnel of snow, his feet pointing down at a forty-five-degree angle.

The bird hopped forward and pecked at the broken lens of his sunglasses. Skydancer stirred.

He opened his eyes and saw the bird.

He tried to move his bruised lips but failed, and then suddenly his muscles responded and he cried out as he became aware of pain.

The bird screamed and bolted into the air, terrified by the sudden noise and movement of something it had thought to be dead.

Skydancer pulled an arm free, amazed to find that it still worked. He began pushing the white powder out from the lip of the hole. The left sleeve of his suit coat was gone. His arm, bare to the shoulder where the shirt had ripped away, was red with welts. The shredded remains of his tie clung to his neck.

Rubbing his arm, he flexed it. At least it wasn't broken. He touched a finger to a puffy eye. His vision was blurry but his eyes seemed to be okay.

He was not fully conscious as he slowly moved his head from side to side, trying to get his bearings. His mind was confused, as if it swam in a sea of pain-filled mist.

In a daze he looked upward toward the sky. What he saw there, the clear blue sky above the mountain, did not seem to register on him.

Pulling free his other hand with some effort, he began to scrape at the packed snow. He felt cramped and uncomfortable and it hurt everywhere. He had to lift himself up somehow.

He tried to lever himself up out of the snow with his hands but the still fastened seat belt held him firmly in place.

He strained to force his hands through the snow down toward his lap. He felt the pressure around his waist and his cold-numbed fingers fumbled with the clasp.

It was a long hard struggle before he heard the snap of the belt releasing. With the strap undone, some of the pain in his lower half eased and he was able to tell as he shifted a little in the hole that his legs still worked.

"Help!" he muttered. His voice was not strong enough to carry. "I'm hurt . . . somebody, please help me!"

Nothing responded to his cry. Dimly, he knew he had to get out of the snow if he was going to survive.

Skydancer dug his fingers in again and pulled his battered body forward a few inches out of the snow. "I'm alive!" he yelled. "Does anybody hear me? I'm alive!"

Bracing his shoeless feet on the seat, he heaved upward, his knees forcing his overcoat up out of his lap and onto the top of the snowbank. His voice broke and he had to fight an overwhelming urge to break into hysterical laughter. Calming himself, he listened for the sounds of rescue he knew must be there.

He heard only the chirping of birds and the rustle of the trees.

Things began suddenly to register, became more clear, and he stared in shock at his surroundings. All around him was rugged and inhospitable mountain terrain. It was as incomprehensible to him as the surface of the moon. City-raised, he had only a small child's memory of wilderness. He looked up and saw the broken and dangling branches of a tree. Surrounding the hole he was in, were more smashed branches and leaves. A part of his mind that was still rational calculated his path of descent through the trees and into the snowbank.

Pulling himself to his feet beside the hole, he inspected his body. For the first time he noticed his wet socks and his frame shook with cold. He unraveled his coat and drew it on, wincing as he scraped his bruised arm through the heavy wool. He buttoned it up to his neck, the collar over his ears. Then he stood there in the leaves and snow, his face blackened and bloody, uncertain what to do.

He knew he would freeze to death if he did not start moving. He wiped at his eyes and began to pick his way tenderly over the rocky ground. Coming out from under the stand of trees, he faced a sparse incline dotted with snow and boulders. He looked up the hill and his gaze centered on an object halfway up the grade. It was black and it stood out against the white background and dun-colored rocks.

He started up the hill and slipped, falling to his knees in the loose rocks. He could see the object clearly now. It was his attaché case.

He scrambled on faster, panting, scraping his already bleeding hands on the hard ground. The case was almost within reach when he stumbled and fell again. His breathing was sharp and painful now and blood streaked his cut face. He stretched out prone and dug his toes into the ground, reaching down for the attaché case. As his fingers touched one corner, he sighed in relief.

It was reachable.

His hand closed on the corner of the case and he began to pull it toward him.

One of the briefcase clasps was broken, the other was loose.

He almost had it when the case snapped open and the papers inside were caught by a stiff breeze. They cascaded out of the case, blew away, up over the hillside, rising and dipping in the wind like a flight of butterflies.

Skydancer threw up his hands in a futile gesture meant to stop the floating papers. They whirled away from his grasping fingers, fluttering irretrievably into a steep-walled gorge. That was it, then.

They were gone.

The briefcase dropped from his fingers, clattering away down toward the bottom of the gorge. It spun on the glassy snow and smashed jarringly against the rocks below.

It was like watching a metaphor of his life unfolding. One fragment of paper soared for a moment on an updraft before it passed out of sight.

He stared at the bottom of the gorge, hating it, hating himself. As Skydancer looked into the depths, the hard stone walls seemed to waver and melt, taking the shape of a hotel room.

"It's our last night together, our last minute together," said Pamela. "If you think I'm kidding, just tear up those papers."

"It isn't right. It doesn't have anything to do with my being Indian or not. It's a question of ethics."

"Harvard taught you ethics?" said Pamela sarcastically. "Somehow I can't imagine the course work. Was that an elective subject or did you figure this out as an extracurricular activity."

Skydancer held the papers in his hand like they were sticks of dynamite. "Harvard didn't teach courses on how to play God. These are human beings we're talking about!"

"What am I, chopped liver?"

"There isn't much radiation danger in Brentwood Estates. You're not exactly in danger, are you?"

"Our marriage is, our life together is," she said coldly.

"Look, I can't make this kind of choice," said Skydancer. "I love you. I love you more than I've ever loved anything in the world."

"Choose me, then," Pamela said, and she came and put her arms around him. She dragged him back onto the bed. He fiercely desired her.

The telephone rang. They kissed passionately. It rang again. She broke away.

"My father. I expected him to call." She reached for the phone, pushing his head aside. As the phone continued to ring, she held the receiver with one hand and looked at him with a question in her eyes.

"Still having a hard time trying to choose?"

Skydancer looked anguished.

"I'll decide for you. I don't want to lose my husband."

She lifted the receiver. "Hello, Father. The papers are signed. Un-huh. Yes. That's right. Handled it like a champion. Right. Yes, John's taking the noon flight to deliver the papers. He'll file the same day he arrives, well before the deadline."

Skydancer got off the bed slowly, his face a mask of conflicting emotions. He walked to the window and stared out at nothing.

"And, Father, what we discussed. Yes, even more so. Try not to be mad but I . . . That's right . . . We're already married."

She made a kissing motion in John's direction and laughed. John kept his back to her.

"Oh, Father, you can't blame me. It's your fault. You tried to teach me to be proper but I grew up just like you."

She laughed again, and tried to catch Skydancer's attention. He did not turn around.

"I knew you'd say yes now. I love you, Dad."

Skydancer turned and looked at her, asking himself if she was worth the price he was about to pay.

Her honey-blond hair was like a silken tent on the pillow. Her eyes, deep and fire-touched, were like blue gems. She was lovely in all kinds of ways, sprawled on the bed, her thin beautiful face alive and animated as she talked gaily to her father. Her skin was flawless, her legs long and wicked and carved out of pearl. She was the most radiantly full-of-life person he had ever met.

He would be lost if he paid the price. A part of him knew it and understood it. And also accepted it. For he would be even more lost without her. A man could only know one such love in a lifetime.

He would pay the price.

She was down there at the bottom of the gorge somewhere. On a few lost squares of paper, neatly signed. On those damned white man's talking leaves.

Skydancer started to laugh.

He'd sold his soul for a blue-eyed blonde who meant everything to him and now he'd lost it all. In a plane wreck on a mountain in the middle of nowhere. In the wind and snow of nowhere.

He laughed hysterically. He felt an irresistible urge to dive into the gorge after the briefcase.

Why not? Supposing he ever got out of here, made it back somehow to civilization, without those papers she'd be gone. Oh, it wasn't his fault. Nobody could blame a plane crash on him. Christ! It was a miracle that he even was still alive.

What they would blame him for would be the shutdown of the uranium mine by the government because the company was going to be liable. A couple hundred million dollars of liable. The lawyers for the other side would be filing in a few days. It was common knowledge.

What they would say about him was that he wasn't a winner. A winner wouldn't have lost the briefcase. A winner wouldn't be in a plane crash. That only happened to losers.

It was over. Skydancer had lost everything.

He edged near the rim of the gorge. His foot loosened a small rock and it went crashing down against the sides of the gorge.

Just one leap, one sickening plunge and a few seconds of pain and that would be it. I could jump right now, he thought.

But that would take courage.

Skydancer was a loser. John Skydancer didn't have any.

Along with ethics, it was something else Harvard hadn't taught him.

17

Red Hawk knelt and stared intently at the tracks in the snow.

What he read there made him even more wary.

Rising, he looked ahead suspiciously to the wall of brush ahead of him. He decided his forward progress was blocked and that he would have to go around. If the cougar was waiting for him in there, he'd get around it and come at it from behind.

Red Hawk hefted his rifle to his shoulder and started up a rise to his right. Halfway up the grade, the ground began angling steeply and he had to pull at bushes and low-hanging tree branches to keep him upright.

After much exertion, he reached the top of the slope. He sighed with weariness and looked down at what lay ahead of him. At his feet stretched a large, secluded valley peppered with drifts of snow amid the dense foliage.

His eyes restlessly swept the valley. He sensed the nearby presence of the black cougar ahead of him somewhere but he saw no sign of it.

Red Hawk gripped the stock of his rifle, raised it in the air and cried: "KIIIIIIIIYIIIIII!"

The warlike cry echoed and reechoed through the mountains.

"I am Red Hawk! I stalk my enemy on Spirit House! I cry the war cry! Come meet me, my enemy!"

Faint echoes were the only answer his challenge got. Again, in the light of day, far from the fear of the night before, Red Hawk was what he had always been.

A killer.

Adjusting his hunter's pack to a more comfortable position on his shoulder, Red Hawk started down into the valley. To his left, on the other side of the rise he had yet to climb, shielded from his line of sight by tall trees, a thin plume of smoke rose into the morning sky.

It marked the grave of a 727.

18

John Skydancer didn't dive into the gorge.

He did something almost as insane.

He climbed down into it. It was a nightmarish effort, a killing task, but Skydancer was not quite sane.

If he were completely lucid, he would quite rightly have been afraid to attempt it.

He had no skill or aptitude for it. Haltingly, despite the odds, he made his way painfully and slowly down the side of the gorge. His bloody hands painted an erratic line down the sharp rock edges of the gorge. Somehow, he reached the bottom.

A little voice in his mind seemed to be saying that a winner would find the briefcase, retrieve the papers and make it back to civilization. A winner. A winner.

Lingering wisps of cloud hovered over the floor of the gorge. The gorge was narrow, steep at both sides and almost flat at its base.

From the direction Red Hawk was coming, the gorge was fairly accessible. Trees grew on the gorge's inner slopes, pushing up and out over the gorge. The leafy giants made the gorge invisible from the air and hardly noticeable at any great distance from the ground.

A stream had once run through the gorge. A wall of stones and limbs, a natural dam that had been built over the years by surging summer waters, had bisected it. On the other side of the blockage, buried in scattered snowdrifts, were several pieces of luggage and jagged scraps of metal.

The plane had broken into two huge sections, one section plunging into the gorge. The section that had contained John Skydancer had fallen on the rim of the gorge, while the rest of the plane plunged past and down into the gorge. It was that lucky accident that had spared Skydancer from the fireball that had incinerated most of the other passengers in the main section of the plane.

On the near side of the dam, nature, untouched by humans, reigned.

Beyond the blocked stream bed was a different world. The ground was black and rutted, littered with the blackened, smoldering remains of flight 193. Scattered over the entire left wall of the gorge and most of its floor was the wreckage of the 727.

The only object that was immediately recognizable as an aircraft part was the plane's horizontal stabilizer, jutting from the top of a snowbank. Pieces of burned and twisted metal clung to its skeletal frame.

Around it, what had been the interior of the passenger compartment was everywhere.

The high sides of the gorge had confined the wreckage in this narrow enclosure, bodies piled on rocks, bushes, sandwiched between broken seats and charred aluminum. A line of crushed luggage marched up the gorge to its end. Some pieces rested far up the end wall, embedded in snow and dirt, embraced by tree limbs.

The ground at the bottom of the gorge was fairly level. Two hundred feet from the main section of the plane, a single suitcase sat alone in a snowbank. It was intact.

It was Skydancer's suitcase.

The sun centered overhead as Skydancer made his way slowly through the brush. His long topcoat was ripped and torn in many places. Damage sustained more in his descent down the gorge wall than in the crash. His socks, once black, were now tinged red with blood. In one hand, he held the shattered remnants of his briefcase. He had one arm wrapped around it to keep it from springing open.

Skydancer's eyes darted over the ground, searching.

Spying a square of white floating in the lower branches of a tree, he limped forward, his eyes wide, frantic. The wind stirred the paper and loosened it. He rushed forward toward his target, tripped and fell, going to his knees on the hard ground under the tree.

Rising in pain, he reached upward, straining to catch the windborne paper with his outstretched hand. His hand batted against the paper, and it curled inward, losing the wind and falling back toward him.

But the wind caught it up again, rushing it past his head, rolling and spinning out of his grasp.

The stiff mountain wind, icy cold, whirled the piece of paper through the trees, skimming the surface of the snow. Skydancer chased the paper, doubled over, stumbling over the rocks in his path.

It was an absurd act as he tramped past the bodies of his dead fellow passengers but Skydancer was self-unaware.

Finally he lunged forward and fell on the paper, bringing it to the ground with his body. Sighing, he reached under his body and tenderly brought forth the paper. It was one of his, the third page of the document. Only twenty more to go.

He opened the case and stuffed the paper inside.

Rising, he held the case tightly to his chest, the way a child holds a stuffed animal when it is afraid of the dark. He resumed his search through the trees.

Skydancer was still in shock, his mind fixed on a reality that had no place where he was. He had to abandon his quest or die. He was in the last stages of exhaustion and it was bitterly cold.

Looking down at his shattered wristwatch, Skydancer cursed and hurried up his pace. The hands of his watch were frozen at the time of the plane's impact.

If I get all the papers and get out of here by tomorrow morning, I can still file by Tuesday, Skydancer told himself. I Have to find them.

I have to find them.

19

The cougar would stand motionless at the top of a ridge just long enough for Red Hawk to get him in his sights. Red Hawk would carefully squeeze off a shot and the cougar would leap away before the bullet hit.

Red Hawk watched the tree line.

Nothing moved.

Readying his rifle, he walked off toward the spot where he had last seen the black cougar. Halfway to the trees, he halted suddenly, lifting his face to the sky.

Over the trees, the drone of a light plane broke the stillness of the mountain.

As Red Hawk stared up, the plane passed a little to the right, the sound of the engine fading in the wind.

In the cockpit of the Cessna, two men in Civil Air Patrol uniforms watched the ground rush by. One man piloted the light plane while the other used binoculars to study the mountain slopes.

The Cessna had passed close enough to Red Hawk so that he could have been seen but the observer was looking in the other direction.

"Better try it to the west. It's a damn big mountain," said the man with the binoculars, rubbing his eyes. "And when you think you've seen it all, there's always another ridge."

The pilot nodded and banked the plane to the west.

A thousand feet below the belly of the Cessna search plane, concealed by heavy foliage in the bottom of the gorge, Skydancer opened his suitcase. He fumbled in the bottom of the bag and came up with a pair of shoes, his second pair for his dark suit.

He gingerly removed his socks, wiping the blood off his bruised and rock-cut feet with a dirty shirt.

He pulled on a clean pair of socks, wincing as the cloth touched abraded flesh. He put the shoes on. His feet were cold. He was cold.

But the important thing for Skydancer was that he had found the papers. All except one page near the middle but a new one could be retyped and reinserted.

It was only after he had found the last paper that he really became aware of the cold.

Skydancer shivered. It seemed like the temperature was dropping.

He rummaged around in his recovered suitcase for something warm to wear but the bag seemed to contain only ties and underwear and toiletries. At the bottom, he found a shirt he didn't remember having packed.

Removing his topcoat, he ripped away what was left of his shirt.

Skydancer groaned as the stiff fabric of the shirt came into contact with welts on his arms and shoulders. Despite the cold, he was sweating. His body seemed to be in shock.

He got the topcoat back on and closed up his suitcase. He hefted it, finding the handle still serviceable.

Skydancer tested his footing on the slick ground. The shoes helped a lot.

He began limping out of the clearing, suitcase in one hand, briefcase under the other arm.

He presented a pathetic cartoonlike figure as he attempted to navigate the slippery ascent out of the gorge, clutching desperately to the things that were his.

He took the side of the gorge that was the least steep, the most accessible, but still it was not an easy clinb. Encumbered as he was, it was even harder.

Twice he lost his balance and slid down an embankment, almost tumbling all the way back down to the bottom of the gorge. But never did he for a second think of relinquishing his hold on the possessions that linked him to the world as he knew it, to the world of deals, houses, cars and money, to the white man's world that had become his world.

Skydancer staggered along through the snow, hunched low against the wind, dragging the dead weight of the huge suitcase.

A man in the middle of a nightmare.

A frightened man trying to hold on to a world that had no place in this other world of wind and wild animals, in the world of Spirit House mountain, that had summoned him as surely as it had summoned another.

20

Skydancer had not eaten since early the previous day and hunger gnawed at his gut like a rat. If possible, he looked worse than he had when he discovered his suitcase.

He dragged the leaden suitcase over the ground as he made his way down the mountainside, moving down below the snow line. Long shadows lay at the bottom of the ravine. He braced himself and slid down the bank in a cloud of dust. His clothes were torn again, covered with grime, and his face wore a haunted look that mirrored the trial he was enduring.

Exhausted, he stumbled to the bottom of the grade, and stopped, unable to go any farther. Sitting with his cases at his side, he braced his back against a tree. He looked back up at the brutal scarps that surrounded the ravine, trying to decide which direction to go.

He was lost. Hopelessly and completely.

Skydancer reached down, scooped up a handful of snow and held it to his mouth. It stuck to his cracked and parched lips, stinging like fire. He wolfed down several handfuls of snow and then rubbed his snowy hands over the bruises on his face. It made his face numb.

The valley was quiet except for wild bird sounds and the buzzing of insects. Skydancer was just at the lower edge of the snow line.

A heavy twig cracked and Skydancer looked up into the tree above him. A large squirrel peered back at him. It watched him for a moment, then scurried back up the tree.

Suddenly a flock of birds rose en masse from the nearest trees.

Skydancer was taken by surprise and threw his hands up over his face, as if warding off a blow.

After the birds had flown, there was silence. Then the unmistakable *crack* of a gunshot.

For a second Skydancer could not believe he had heard it. He inclined his head, straining to hear. He was rewarded by the sound of another shot, this time sounding even closer.

Jumping up, he grabbed his bags and ran out from under the tree.

"Over here!" he shouted weakly. "Somebody! . . . Over here!"

His voice did not carry far in the thickly wooded forest. He coughed and cleared his throat. "Is anybody there?" he yelled. "Hey! I'm over here! Help! Help!"

He kept running.

The sudden strain was too much for him. His legs gave out suddenly and he collapsed in a fit of coughing. When the spasm passed he lay there, drenched in sweat. Then he heard the third shot, much farther away than the others. He forced himself to rise with a strength of will he did not know he possessed. Dragging his cases, he stumbled off in the direction of the gunfire.

On a stretch of level ground he ducked a rock overhang and ran out into the trees. Near a sheer drop-off the suitcase snagged on a rock and he was pulled back violently, almost going over into the abyss below. The case was caught. He yanked on it. It jerked loose, sending him sprawling to the ground.

The hasps of the suitcase ruptured, scattering clothes everywhere. Skydancer frantically tried to recapture his tumbled possessions. On his hands and knees, he tried to restuff them into his broken bag, his hands reaching and grabbing. A part of his mind became aware of how ridiculous this all was.

It was almost as if a part of his mind was saying he would not be rescued unless he was properly dressed. An absurdity, but his mind was clouded with fears and anxieties almost overwhelming.

Skydancer tried to close the broken case and only partially succeeded. With the briefcase under one arm, he hugged the suitcase to his chest and began a stumbling run up the side of the hill. He got exactly ten feet.

The suitcase thumped by his pumping knees burst like a rotten pumpkin, squirted out of his grasp and sent Skydancer's clothes cascading over a ledge.

The wind caught the contents of the bag and Skydancer's clothes bobbed up and down like sea gulls in a storm.

He lunged desperately at the suitcase, trying to stop it from going over, but succeeded in only twisting his knee on the uneven ground and went crashing painfully and heavily against the rocks.

The sudden pain stopped Skydancer cold. He just lay there on his side, not moving, and for the first time saw the futility of what he was trying to do. He was exhausted.

He closed his eyes and lay there like a condemned prisoner awaiting execution.

I can't run another step, thought Skydancer. I'm going to die here. I'm not going to be rescued.

I'm going to die in the mountains like a wild Indian, he thought, and it seemed laughable. And then he corrected it. No, like a tame Indian, his battered mind said. A wild Indian would know how to survive here.

21

The sun was setting as Red Hawk picked his way through a ravine. He held his rifle upright, moving quietly over the snow-covered ground, his eyes prowling for danger on all sides.

He moved in a hunter's crouch, his attention fixed on a movement in the trees ahead of him. It was too far away to see clearly, so Red Hawk lifted the gun and squinted through the scope.

Low-hanging branches obscured his vision. He lowered the rifle and moved on cautiously. At the end of the ravine his path was blocked by a rock outcropping. Bending, he ducked under it and circled around. Using the rock as cover, he stopped, cocked his gun and listened.

He didn't hear anything and it worried him. Something strange had passed through here, that was evident.

He began to edge slowly around the rock, the rifle held in readiness. He jumped, gun out and targeted at the brush from which the movement had come.

He stared, his mouth hanging open in surprise. Red Hawk lowered the rifle.

"What the hell?"

Red Hawk moved to the bush, used the barrel of his gun to pry something out of the bush and took it in his hand.

He turned a brightly colored tie over in his hand, frowning. Its appearance here was as surprising as if Red Hawk had suddenly come upon a dead elephant.

At the top of the ravine, Skydancer lay on his side, waiting to die. The two men were within a hundred yards of each other.

It might as well have been a hundred miles.

22

Red Hawk threw the tie away and retraced his steps back down the ravine. On a ledge, two hundred yards above, the cat watched him. It also looked down on Skydancer sitting near the top of the ravine. Red Hawk moved down the cut, going farther away from the defeated Skydancer. The cat focused its yellow eyes on Skydancer and growled.

It began its descent to lower ground. Coming out of the brush at the base of the cliff, it stopped and studied the hunched figure with its face buried in its arms. It growled again, softly. Turning its head, it could see Red Hawk disappearing into the trees at the other end of the ravine. The cat turned, disappearing into the trees as well.

It went after Red Hawk, ignoring Skydancer.

The campfire was set between two large logs twenty feet apart. The moon was obscured by the tall peaks. The only light came from the fire as it spilled light and shadow on the trees. Red Hawk knelt near the fire, feeding the blaze with small branches. Satisfied that it would burn for some time, he rose and walked to his backpack, sitting upright against one of the logs.

He looked down at it and grunted. Bending, he tucked the straps down the front so they would be out of sight. Removing his coat, he settled it around the pack. Red Hawk shivered as the cold mountain air penetrated his deerskin shirt. Finding a small straight twig, he wedged it upright in the top of the pack. He took off his battered black hat and set it on the twig. Taking his rifle from the top of the log, he placed it across the front of the pack and braced it with a small rock.

He walked around the makeshift dummy. From the rear and in the flickering firelight, it took on the semblance of a sitting man. He smiled.

Red Hawk kicked more wood into the fire, then walked to a tree outside the circle of light. He agilely climbed to a fork in the branches about ten feet above the ground. From there he could look directly down on the coat-covered backpack in the center of the clearing. He settled in, making himself as comfortable as possible in the cramped space. He shivered in the bitter cold.

Reaching into his belt, he removed the .45 automatic. He pulled the slide back and let it snap into place, loading a shell into the chamber. In the ruddy firelight the sly cunning that made Red Hawk one with the animal he hunted was more than apparent. He surveyed the trap.

Now all he could do was wait. An hour later he began to doze, the bitter cold sapping his strength. The fire had lost much of its original brilliance but still burned high enough to light the space beneath the tree with an eerie glow. Red Hawk nodded forward, catching himself on the edge of sleep. Wiping at his eyes, he squirmed in the fork of the tree. He was beginning to freeze.

The only sound was that of the crackling fire. His eyelids fell and he began to breathe deeper, more rhythmically. Suddenly, he caught his breath and his eyes snapped open.

Nothing moved.

There was no sound in the clearing save for the fire. But something was there. Red Hawk knew that as sure as he knew his name. His grip tightened on the pistol.

A bush moved behind the dummy.

Red Hawk smiled, anticipating success. He raised his pistol in both hands and held it out, centered on the bush. The movement stopped. Red Hawk remained poised. His smile dissolved when he heard the scraping noise from below and behind.

He turned his head slightly but the position of his body prevented him from bringing the gun full around.

Another noise and movement, this time to his extreme right. He leaned that way, then a bush creaked from his left. On the verge of panic, he swung the gun back and forth, almost losing his balance.

He grabbed at a limb to steady himself. The cat had the power of spirits and Red Hawk's fear rose.

The darkness closed in on him like a suffocating blanket. The muscles in his throat constricted and his jaw went slack. For one of the very few times in his life he was utterly terrified, terrified of things he had never believed in.

Another noise. This time a snarl of hatred from below and behind again. The cat was circling him, purposely trying to confuse and anger him. He tried to look down but in his panic it seemed like a drop of a thousand feet to the ground.

On the other side of the dummy, away from the tree holding Red Hawk, the cat hugged the ground, now silent. Its heavy breathing rivaled the crackling of the fire but Red Hawk's nerves were raw and he heard neither. From the tree limb he fired a shot down into the clearing.

The shot shook the trees. The cat stayed put, watching.

He fired again, at the lurking black shadow. "I'll kill you!" he yelled. "Come on! Come and get it!"

The cat obliged him.

It rose from the brush in a gigantic leap and sailed into the clearing. Red Hawk heard the breaking of bushes and struggled to turn himself in the tree. He looked down at the fire and pure horror seized him like the jaws of death.

The clearing was unchanged. The cat was nowhere in sight and the dummy sat in the exact same position Red Hawk had left it. The ground around the fire was undisturbed.

Except for one small detail.

The rifle was gone.

23

The parking lot of Northpass's one and only supermarket was ablaze with lights.

Telephone poles had been strung with emergency spotlights and the white-lined pavement was bright as day. In the center of the lot, a helicopter squatted, its blades rotating slowly until they stopped. Air Force trucks lined the highway leading to the market.

Regulars from Cheyenne Mountain and Colorado Springs amiably joked with National Guardsmen as they leaned on jeeps, lounging in the glare of the floodlights.

A mobile command post had been set up in a trailer at the entrance to the market. Groups of CAP and Air Force officers studied maps pinned to the outside of the trailer. The sleepy out-of-the-way settlement had become a hive of activity.

Sheriff Fiske's jeep entered the lot, snaked through a line of State Police cars and pulled up in front of the command trailer. The sheriff looked around at the milling soldiers as he left the jeep and stepped up into the trailer. Inside the trailer was an even larger and more chaotic jumble of soldiers and staff personnel.

"Sheriff! Over here." The man beckoning Fiske was Colonel Abe Tucker, an Air Force officer from Colorado Springs. Fiske maneuvered through the swarm of people at tightly packed tables that ran down the middle of the trailer. They met in front of a large plotting board that took up one inside wall of the command post.

Tucker, an intense man on the wrong side of middle age, stopped tapping the wall map with a pointer he held in his hand and aimed the slender stick at Fiske. "Gentlemen," he said to the three others who had been the object of his briefing, "this is Sheriff Fiske. If anybody knows these mountains better than he does, he was probably raised by wolves up above the snowpack."

Fiske nodded a self-conscious hello. The three men were dressed in civilian clothes and had an outdoors look about them. "Lloyd, these are the heads of the ground search units." Tucker rattled off the names but Fiske didn't pay much attention until he heard Frank Scanlon, and was shaking the hand of the burly forest ranger.

"We've met," said Scanlon to the colonel. "About a year ago when that little girl was lost. How are you, Lloyd?"

Fiske remembered Scanlon, who had spearheaded the search party through the rugged mountains and had single-handedly found and carried out the twelve-year-old who had been lost for thirty hours. Fiske smiled, nodding to Scanlon as the colonel turned, tapping the map.

"Let me show you what we're up against here." The map was crisscrossed with red tape and grease-penciled circles. Fiske frowned and rubbed his jaw. "This is where contact was lost with the aircraft." Tucker indicated a point at the northern tip of the map. "This line shows the direction it was traveling at the last reported radar sighting. This area has already been covered by air search . . . Aerial photos are being developed right now and we should have them within the hour. As you know, on the first go-through we found nothing, no trace of wreckage.

"Unless the photos turn up something we missed we're going to have to cover this area." He made a sweeping gesture that took in three-quarters of the lower section of the map. "By ground search."

Fiske looked at Scanlon and whistled. Scanlon smiled back.

"You'll need an army," said Fiske.

"You're right," Tucker reluctantly admitted. "That's why we need your help. I want you to go over the map with these unit commanders and brief them on what kind of terrain they can expect to encounter at this time of year."

"Bad," grunted Scanlon.

"I'll drink to that," echoed Fiske.

Tucker frowned, the creases on his face beginning to resemble the map on the wall. "I'm afraid that's true. In any case, I'd appreciate it if you'd take a look at the photos and give them any help or advice you can."

Fiske took the pointer from Tucker's hand and aimed it at the map. "Here, and here, almost impassable until the snowpack melts some, maybe three, four weeks." He had indicated the high mountain range to the northwest. Then he moved the pointer down to the valleys that approached Northpass. "This here's pretty accessible—but she didn't go in there or you'da seen her from the air."

He touched the high peaks directly north with the rubber tip. "This is where you'll find 'er, if you find 'er at all."

"How long do you figure it'd take for us to get there?" asked one of the watching men.

Fiske shook his head. "Two, maybe three days, if the weather holds. Two, maybe three months, if it don't."

An airman entered carrying a packet of photographs and handed them to Tucker. The colonel thumbed through them quickly. "Okay, Lloyd, they're all yours," he said, handing them to Fiske. "I got two dozen other things I should be doing." He nodded at the others, starting to move off into the crowd.

Fiske held up his hand. "Before you go, I got something to tell you. Another problem possibly."

Tucker turned and looked. "Just what we need."

"Yesterday one of my prisoners got the drop on me, stole some guns, ammo and supplies and headed up into these mountains."

"Well, that's not going . . ." started Tucker.

"I ain't finished," said Fiske. "He's an Indian. And he's a killer, plain and simple. That's what he was in jail for. Murder."

"His name is . . ." He was cut off abruptly.

Tucker turned to the airman who had brought the photographs. "Send word, everybody who goes up carries a gun. That's an order!"

The airman saluted, turned and rushed off.

"Frankly, Sheriff," snapped Tucker, "you couldn't have picked a worse time or place to lose a prisoner. Do you consider him dangerous? Will he interfere with the search?"

"Dangerous? Yes. He'd kill without blinking an eye. As to his interfering, I don't think so. He was born and raised in the mountains. He'll think he's being pursued, so he'll hide as only an Indian can hide. I don't think anybody is even gonna get close to him."

"We'll handle it, Sheriff." Tucker made as if to leave again.

"One other thing," said Lloyd Fiske. "My prisoner is chasing a black cougar. It's got to be all of fourteen foot long, black as coal and absolute poison to tangle with. It's already killed a horse and a colt. Would kill a man if it got too close."

Tucker laughed. "I've seen mountain lions. We've got enough guns to scare off any of the wild animals."

Fiske shrugged. "If you say so. All I know is, a cougar big enough to bite a full-grown mare's head off is big enough to give anybody trouble who tangles with him."

Tucker handed Fiske the aerial photographs. "Look these over with my men. And, Sheriff, let's not borrow any trouble we don't have to. We've got enough problems with inexperienced men without bringing in escaped Indian killers and wild cougars. I'd appreciate it if you'd keep the cougar story under your hat. I'm having enough trouble getting volunteers to go up as it is and we need every man we can get."

Fiske nodded. "It's your show."

After Fiske had gone over the pictures with the men, he and Ranger Scanlon stood outside the trailer smoking and watching the three-ring circus take shape. Scanlon blew a smoke ring at the mountains and said, "The good colonel gave me ten green cadets from the Academy to make up my group. Half of 'em never been on a horse before. They're going to be worthless, if they even get that good. Don't suppose I could talk you into riding up with my group? Sure would make the babysitting a lot easier."

Fiske knocked the ash off the end of his cigarette and smiled.

"Sure. Why not. If things get too dull I can tell your greenies about the cougar and have the fun of watching them lift their skirts and paddle frantically for home."

"That cougar as bad as you say?" asked Scanlon.

"Worse. Don't think there's a cougar like it anywhere in the world. Pure poison."

Scanlon crushed out his cigarette with a laugh. He feigned terror. "Now that you've talked me out of going, I guess you'll have to lead my group. That prisoner, Red Hawk?"

"You know about it?"

Scanlon nodded. "Read the paper. Knew him too. I'm surprised the son of a bitch is still alive. I figured somebody must have surely stuck a knife in him by now. He's too mean to live."

Fiske grinned around his cigarette. "Frank, my grandpappy taught me never to criticize anybody that mean."

"Your grandpappy? Wasn't he the one that was killed in that bar fight with a drunken lumberjack who was about six sizes bigger than he was?"

Fiske nodded. "Yeah, well I never said he practiced what he preached."

Scanlon laughed heartily. Fiske smiled at the other man's reaction and looked up at the mountain. His thoughts touched on Red Hawk and the black cougar, two killers moving against each other up there somewhere on the mountain.

"I wonder who's killing who?" he said.

Skydancer sat on the cold ground and pulled his coat tight against his shivering frame. He stared blankly at the darkness that surrounded him. He had never felt quite so alone in his life. The darkness around him seemed filled with dangers, all the more horrible because he could not see them. A rustling noise in the bushes caused him to moan. He was a totally destroyed city dweller in the midst of a jungle he felt sure he would never leave. He was convinced he was going to die on the mountain. He had no idea where he was or in which direction to walk to get back to civilization. I'm one hell of an Indian, he thought to himself.

He shivered with the cold and thought: My ancestors are probably spinning on their burial racks. He knew he ought to be making a better show of it but he was scared and cold and hungry and he was hurt, goddamnit.

He had no idea how to make a shelter or how to obtain food or build a fire. He had none of the wilderness skills of the people of his own tribe. He really did not think of himself as an Indian. He certainly knew very little about it. He had seen more Indians in movies than he had in real life.

He put a hand to his dirt-streaked face. His jaw ached. He must have struck it in the crash. Every part of him seemed to ache. His face mirrored the despair and helplessness he felt.

The sound of a shot snapped him bolt upright. A tiny ray of hope gleamed in his eyes. Painfully he crawled to the edge of the ridge and looked down into the blackness of the gorge below. At the end of the gorge the echo of the shot blended into the crack of another, then faded away. Skydancer saw the light of a campfire. "Thank you . . . thank you . . ." he croaked through blistered lips. He got to his feet and, half stumbling, half running, rushed down the loose slate of the hillside. He tripped and fell, tumbling head first, bringing up his briefcase to protect his face. He slid to the bottom, rose haltingly, stumbling toward the light in the woods. He held the battered case high, beating back the low branches that blocked his way.

He was less than quiet as he stumbled against branches, fighting the attacking limbs, staggering onward. He fell again, crawled a few feet, then rose to go on.

"Wait this time . . . Please wait . . ."

His voice was only a gasping animal sound that did not carry far. "Don't go away . . . I'm coming . . ."

The light from the fire grew steadily nearer but Skydancer was exhausted and his steps faltered. He used the low branches as crutches to help him toward his goal. He was almost to the circle of firelight when he came abreast of a large tree.

As he passed the tree something massive sprang from the shadows and landed on the path in front of him.

Skydancer screamed and brought his case up to shield his face.

Red Hawk stood crouched on the trail, legs wide apart, pistol extended in both hands, pointing at Skydancer's chest. "What the hell?" exclaimed Red Hawk, as surprised as the man he had almost shot.

Skydancer looked at the rugged, chill-beaten figure of the Indian for a moment. He reached out a hand toward him. He opened his mouth to speak but passed out, falling in the snow at Red Hawk's feet.

Red Hawk followed the body to the ground with the muzzle of the gun. "What the hell?" he repeated as he stared at the prone figure before him.

24

The long black limo threaded its way through the foggy San Francisco streets. At the wheel, Skyler Tannerman, Pamela's father, handled the car clumsily. He had dismissed the chauffeur for carelessness only the day before and hadn't yet had a chance to replace him.

Skyler watched droplets of mist trace a mosaic on the windshield. He liked San Francisco's almost nightly fog. It cleaned the streets and gave them a fresh, untainted appearance.

It was a worried man who pushed the limo through the foggy streets. Worried and apprehensive.

Being a parent in a time of crisis wasn't exactly one of his strengths. Running a multimillion-dollar law firm, that was one of his strengths, not shoring up grief-stricken daughters who were newly married and newly widowed almost within the same week.

It had been several days now and he had only spoken to Pamela once, a short, strained phone call that had left him with a hollow feeling in the pit of his stomach.

He turned onto Thirty-fourth Avenue and parked in front of a large two-bedroom condo that he had given Pamela on her twenty-first birthday.

He pulled up into the driveway. Her blue Porsche was partially blocking the drive. Another car, a red Fiat, which he didn't recognize, was in front of her car. The back of his limo was sticking out on the street.

Locking his car, he turned the collar of his raincoat up around his ears and walked to the front door. He waited a few moments, staring at the building that he had been in only twice before.

Some doting parent I've been, he thought as he rang the bell.

Pamela opened the door a crack, looked out but made no effort to unfasten the chain.

"Hello, Dad. It's late. I didn't expect you."

"I thought, if there's anything I can do . . . maybe we should talk."

She turned and looked back over her shoulder. "Okay, sure," she said but she didn't look enthusiastic.

She closed the door, reopening it without the chain. Skyler followed her down a narrow hallway into the living room. It was an expensively and tastefully furnished apartment.

There were expensive lithos on the wall, Miró, Degas and two Dalis. Also a small oil painting by Picasso.

He sat down awkwardly on an overstuffed chair. She was dressed in a night robe, rather sheer and semi-revealing.

"I was in bed. Can I get you a drink."

"No, thanks."

There was an awkward silence. She seemed very uncomfortable.

"How are you holding up?"

"I'm surviving. I make an attractive widow, don't you think?" There was some emotion in her voice but her father could not read it.

"I'm sorry about Skydancer."

"Yeah."

Pamela sat across from him in a matching chair. He stared at her, not knowing quite what to say. She avoided his gaze, staring into the fireplace, where a fake log burned on a fake fire, shedding a spurious warmth.

"Anything official yet?"

"You mean, have they found his body? No."

Her father picked up a crystal ashtray from a side table and turned it in his hands. "I don't know what to say, Pamela."

"He's dead. That would do for openers. Maybe you could say, 'Tough luck, kid, but it's for the best.' I couldn't tell Skydancer how angry you were on the phone. You hated the idea that we were married. You didn't say it, not in so many words, but I knew. I knew."

"I won't lie to you. I didn't think he was good enough for you. But I'm sorry he's dead."

Pamela lit a cigarette with a gold lighter from the coffee table. "Sorry he's dead or sorry the deal's dead?"

Skyler sighed. He had raised a tough kid. She reminded him of himself, too much like him for her own good.

"Of course, you can't be sure he's dead . . . at least not yet."

Pamela shifted her eyes from the fireplace and centered them on her father's well-fed, clean-shaven face. "Joint checking account closed. Balance zero. Permanently retired from the firm."

"Please, Pamela."

Pamela narrowed her eyes and raised her voice. "What do you care? You ought to be relieved. Now you don't have to carry him anymore. No more favors for me. You can go back to lily white and uptight." Her voice rose until she was almost shouting. "Goddamn you anyway!"

Skyler sighed again and his body seemed to sink down into the chair. He looked old and tired.

A bedroom door opened and a man in a bathrobe, still damp from the shower, stuck his head into the room.

"Hey! What's all the shouting about? You okay, Pamela? This old guy bothering you?"

Skyler was shocked. Pamela saw the look on his face and smiled bitterly.

"It's exactly what you think," she said to her father, and then she turned and called back to the man in the bathrobe, "It's my father. No problem, Michael. I'll be in as soon as I can."

"Okay, then . . . uh, nice to meet you," said Michael, and he went back out the door, a sullen, suspicious look on his face.

"His body isn't even cold," said Skyler.

"So I'm a tramp."

"I thought you loved him! Christ! You married him!" Skyler was angry. "What kind of . . . slut . . ." He stopped suddenly, as he realized it was a word he did not mean to say.

Pamela laughed at him.

"If you could see your face, you'd die."

"What's so funny?" he snapped at her, on the point of losing his temper altogether.

"You being moral all of a sudden. You haven't got a moral bone in your body and there you sit coming across like Sunday night at an evangelism camp-out."

Pamela stubbed her cigarette out in an ashtray. She got up.

"Let me tell you something, Father, before you go. And it is time for you to go. Maybe I loved Skydancer. I don't know. I'd like to think I did. Maybe that's why I married him. Maybe. But I know one thing. I know exactly what kind of person I am. I'm like you, Father. I get what I want when I want it. I've got appetites, Father, just like you've got. I crave power. I like to dominate people. I've got all the vices and no reason not to indulge them. Just like you, Father."

He started to speak but she cut him off.

"Don't say anything, Father. Let me finish. Skydancer was going to be my reason not to indulge all my vices. I hoped that's what he was going to be. Now he's dead. And I'm back to being what I've always been. A rich bastard's slut of a daughter."

"I didn't do a very good job raising you, Pamela. I'm sorry."

"Why should you be sorry? You did a good job. I'm just like you."

Skyler stood up. "I've got a plane to catch early tomorrow morning. Call me if you need anything," he said, tight-lipped.

"Michael and I will be on the same plane tomorrow."

"Why?" Skyler was amazed.

Pamela enjoyed the look of shock on his face.

"You don't even know where I'm going. Why would you want to travel anywhere with me?"

"I know where you're going, that's why. You should fire your new secretary. She may be great to chase around your office but she's a mercenary little bitch. She takes bribes. You're going up to look for your precious papers. Sift through the crash wreckage in a last-ditch effort to save your precious stinking uranium deal. Well, I'm going along for the ride. The least I can do for the poor bastard is bring him home and bury him. It's, well, I owe him that much anyway."

"We owe him that much," agreed Skyler. "Shall I see to the flight arrangements for you . . . and for your friend too? Is that what you'd like?"

She shrugged. "Do what you like. I'm going up there with or without your help."

"I'll take care of it, then," he said, and she got up without another word and went back into the bedroom.

Skyler got up slowly, feeling a million years old and evil and somehow burned out.

He walked to his limo, unlocked it and got in.

She's just like me, he thought as he drove away. That's the way I've raised her.

Christ! He wondered if anybody had ever done as badly as a parent as he had. He doubted it.

25

Red Hawk dragged Skydancer's limp body to the fireside. He unceremoniously propped the unconscious man up against a log.

Skydancer still clutched the attaché case to his chest in a death grip. Red Hawk leaned over and slapped him across the face several times. "Hey, come on, wake the hell up!"

Skydancer groaned, letting the case slip to the ground. His eyelids fluttered. Red Hawk picked up a canteen and poured water into a metal cup. He extended the cup to the confused man before him. Skydancer grabbed at it, spilling half the contents. He gulped the water, then greedily extended the cup. "More?"

Red Hawk poured again. This time Skydancer drank slowly, savoring the cool liquid. "More, please?"

Red Hawk grunted, filling the cup again. "Look, friend, we're twenty-five miles from the nearest road, maybe fifty from a town . . ." He studied Skydancer's clothes. "Care to tell me jus' what the hell you're doing wanderin' around out here in the middle of nowhere dressed like that?"

Skydancer stuck out the cup again but Red Hawk brushed it aside roughly. "I asked you a question, friend."

"You wouldn't have anything to eat, would you? I haven't eaten since . . . sometime yesterday . . . I think."

Red Hawk glared at the pathetic figure before him. "Might have a bit of jerky left. If your city stomach can stand it. I'll let you try it. You got any money? Always charge the tourists for everything. My number one rule." He spat on the ground.

Red Hawk stared at Skydancer's face. "You're real dark for a white boy. What are you, a Mexican or what?"

For the first time, Skydancer looked, really looked at Red Hawk. Almost as if it had just happened or had not been true until now, Skydancer said, "I'm an Indian. Hey!" Skydancer's face lit up momentarily as if claiming his past somehow made him fit in. "You're Indian too. Aren't you? What nation? I'm a . . ."

"Bullshit. Ain't no Indian dresses like that. Cough up the money, tourist!"

Wearily Skydancer leaned against the log, defeated, letting the cup fall to his lap. He was confused by Red Hawk's hostility.

"Tourist? Money? I didn't . . . I don't know." He patted his pockets absentmindedly. "Must have lost my billfold . . . I don't remember having any . . ." He reached for his trouser pockets. "Uh, I might have some change."

"Oh, the hell with it," said Red Hawk in disgust. "I'll feed you, but first you tell me what the hell you're doing up here on Spirit House mountain. I damn sure know you aren't up here looking for me. Not dressed like that. You escape from a nuthouse or what?"

"On Spirit House mountain? This is Spirit House mountain?"

"Hell, no!" Red Hawk said sarcastically. "This is downtown Denver. I'm the mayor and this here's"—he waved the .45 under Skydancer's nose—"the key to the city!"

Skydancer backed away from the gun in his face. He tried to press himself back into the log. In a dim sort of way he understood that Red Hawk was close to blowing his head off but he was still too traumatized by the plane wreck to react.

"You better tell me what you're doing up here or I might just decide to use this." He pressed the gun barrel into Skydancer's forehead.

Skydancer spoke in quick, disjointed sentences.

"I was in the plane . . . an explosion . . . can't remember . . . impact . . . then I was in the snow . . . woke up in my seat . . . what was left of it. Don't know when it happened . . . time . . . lost all track of it. Walked a long time . . . so long. Heard shots this morning . . . tried to find the source but got lost. Too weak . . . must be in shock . . . heard them again tonight . . . saw the fire." His shoulders sagged. "So tired."

The anger on Red Hawk's face turned to interest.

"Plane? What plane?"

"Left San Francisco last night . . . or was it the night before? So hard to remember. Flight to Denver." Skydancer spotted his case next to the log and reached for it, pulling it to his chest. His face looked odd, distorted in the firelight. "I'm . . . I'm late for a meeting. You . . . you've got to help me get to Denver. It's important I don't . . . I . . ."

He shook his head as if trying to clear it. "Feel so strange."

"What kind of plane?" Red Hawk insisted. "Heard a light plane a while back."

"No, large passenger plane . . . big jet . . . crashed . . . all dead . . . only one left . . . bodies . . . so tired." Skydancer's head fell on his chest. He was unable to stay awake.

Red Hawk jabbed the barrel of his pistol into Skydancer's chest, knocking him backwards. Skydancer's eyes snapped open, panic in his face. For a second he relived the fall of the plane until his eyes focused on the man standing above his sprawled body.

"I ain't finished talking," sneered Red Hawk. "How many you figure were on board?"

Skydancer shook his head. "Don't know . . . All dead. Women, children. Everyone."

Red Hawk leaned forward and slapped him. Skydancer's head snapped back. "Goddamnit! How many?"

Skydancer recoiled from the blow. The pain of the slap seemed to restore his sanity somewhat. He stared up at Red Hawk, aware of the question. "I don't know. Maybe two hundred, almost booked solid. However many people the big jets hold, I guess."

Red Hawk stared into the trees, lost in thought. "Over two hundred, huh?" He began digging in his backpack.

Skydancer did not answer again. Red Hawk came out of his pack with a long strip of dried beef. Skydancer felt a dull ache in his side, in his gut. The sight of food made him salivate. He was starved.

Red Hawk tore the strip near one end and then handed the small piece to Skydancer. The man with the gun suddenly seemed friendly. "My name's Red Hawk. Chew on this."

Skydancer snatched at the meat and bit into it eagerly. He spoke around the food. "Thank you, Red Hawk." Stuffing the small piece of meat in his mouth, he put out a dirty hand. "John Skydancer."

Red Hawk stared at the outstretched hand as if it were a poisonous snake.

"Eat your beef," said Red Hawk, turning his back on him.

"Thanks anyway," said Skydancer, letting his hand drop.

Skydancer gulped the dried meat down, nearly choking on the tough strip of jerky. Red Hawk tossed another log on the fire.

"What were you shooting at?" asked Skydancer, curious now that his hunger was partially satisfied.

Red Hawk spun around, his face alive with hate in the firelight.

"A black catunjah! I'd swear the bastard walks with evil spirits! Been tracking him forty miles now." Red Hawk looked grimly at his .45. "I'll kill him or he'll kill me."

He only had a few shells left.

Skydancer's eyebrows lifted. "Uh, catunjah?"

"Mountain lion, cougar." Red Hawk shot a glance to the trees around them. "An evil spirit of this mountain if you believe the kind of crap my old man believes."

"As a child I used to hear stories . . . the old tales . . . but that was a million years ago . . . in another lifetime."

"You still claim you're Indian?" asked Red Hawk disinterestedly.

"I guess not. I could have been once, maybe, but I . . . outgrew it." Skydancer stared at the trees around them, feeling very much in a world that had never really been his. He shivered. "Do you think we're safe? From the cougar? With the fire and all?"

Red Hawk laughed, a flat humorless bark. "Until he figures out how to use the rifle."

"What?"

"Yeah, we're safe enough. I don't think he'll try to take on the two of us . . . at least not tonight. You see any sign of him?"

Skydancer's head was falling toward his chest, exhaustion taking its toll. "Uh, who?"

"The cat, damnit!" Red Hawk kicked another log into the fire. "Forget it. I can see you're gonna be a lot of help."

"Sorry," murmured Skydancer as Red Hawk built the fire into a roaring blaze. "You'll help me, won't you?" asked Skydancer. "The meeting in Denver. Very important. I *have* to get there."

Red Hawk turned away from the fire, pointing a twig at his guest. "Look here. Tomorrow morning you just show me where that plane went in and we'll take it from there."

"I never saw the plane. I have no idea where it might be. There's no way I could lead you . . ."

Red Hawk cut him off. "Don't worry, we'll just backtrack your trail. I don't think we'll have much trouble finding *that.*"

"But why? They're dead. There's nothing we can do. And I really have to get to Denver," Skydancer insisted.

"Well, I ain't holdin' out hope for no other survivors, that's a fact, but we should at least take a look. Mark the spot so we can report the position when we get back. I figure there'll be a big reward. Least we can do," said Red Hawk. He had no intention of going back. Nor did he intend to mark the position of the downed plane. He had something else in mind.

Skydancer's head began to droop, his chin touching his chest. His eyes closed. He was on the verge of total exhaustion. Red Hawk busied himself at the fire. "Figure it can't be too far. You couldn't have covered much ground in your condition. And you ain't exactly dressed for mountain climbing either, are you?" jeered Red Hawk.

Skydancer did not reply. Red Hawk came over to stand above him, listening to his deep breathing. Making sure Skydancer was asleep, he pried the attaché case from his hands, loosening his grip so as not to wake him. "Let's see what you got in here makes you hold on to it so careful. Maybe you got a lot of money in here, huh?" He lifted the case and opened it.

"Nothing."

He spat into the fire as he thumbed through a few scraps of paper. Disgusted, he added them to the fire.

Dropping the case to the ground beside him, he stared down at the sleeping man. "Well, Mr. Skydancer of San Francisco, you rest easy, hear? If you survive the night, come sunup we'll go find us an airplane."

He wrapped his charred blanket around Skydancer and gestured to the same tree he had battled the cat from. "If you need me, I'll be in that tree over there, sort of keeping an eye on things." He moved to the tree, grabbed a lower limb and began hoisting himself up. He stopped to look back at Skydancer, propped up against the log, plainly visible in the firelight. A clear target for the cougar.

"If we get any visitors, you be sure to call out, now, hear?" Red Hawk laughed as he settled himself halfway up in the tree.

At midnight it began to snow.

26

By dawn the snow flurries had subsided but the low overcast effectively eliminated any further air search, at least for the rest of the day. At 9 A.M. a trident of ground units forked out from Northpass, making their way over the loose snow toward the heart of Spirit House mountain.

At the same time, Pamela Skydancer, her companion, Michael, and her father were landing at Stapleton Airport in Denver. They picked up their baggage and Skyler rented a car from the Hertz booth in the lobby. They drove to the Holiday Inn, where they took two adjoining suites. Pamela spent half an hour on the phone checking with the local authorities, who would only tell her that the search was being broadened and results should be forthcoming soon.

Skyler left to make a seemingly endless series of emergency business calls with the promise that they would all drive up to Northpass later that afternoon.

Pamela sat drinking tequila in her suite, while Michael slept, exhausted from lovemaking. She was trying not to think about how quickly Michael had become boring. She couldn't even remember his last name and didn't care if she ever knew it. God, he was about as handsome as he was stupid.

She drank and stared out the window at the mountains.

On one of them, two men made their way upward along the side of a ridge. Red Hawk was in the lead, navigating the rocky grade with ease. Skydancer trailed, suffering at the exertion. Red Hawk, carrying his pistol ready in one hand, stopped often to peer at the ground. Skydancer took advantage of these short stops to catch his breath.

The two men passed under a jutting rock ledge and Red Hawk ducked his head smoothly. Skydancer was looking down wearily at his feet. He hit his head, almost dropping his briefcase.

"Damnit!" For the first time he expressed real anger.

Red Hawk said, "If you'd get rid of that damn briefcase, it'd be easier to climb."

Skydancer clutched the precious case to his chest. "It's my problem. I'm not asking you to carry it."

Red Hawk laughed at the show of bad temper from his ward. "Suit yourself. Just keep up." He pointed at the terrain ahead. "This ain't no Boy Scout hike."

Skydancer lowered his head and ducked under the overhang.

Red Hawk continued to climb, Skydancer close behind, holding tightly on to the briefcase.

Their campsite of the previous night was far behind them now at the bottom of the ridge. The fire had been smothered with snow and a few scraps of paper were all that was left to show that anybody had been there. Several empty cartridge cases gleamed in the snow. The clearing was quiet.

On the log where the dummy had been propped the night before, the cat stretched. Its long body completely covered the big log. It scraped its claws on the bark and looked up at the top of the ridge, barely visible through the trees. Stepping down from the log, it circled the dead campfire. It stopped at the twin set of tracks leading toward the ridge. It emitted a deep growl, its lips pulled back, exposing razor-sharp fangs. It moved forward, following their tracks.

An hour later found the two men on fairly level ground making good time. The sky had cleared somewhat and splotches of sunlight bathed the treetops.

Red Hawk still held the lead, nimbly avoiding fallen logs and small rocks.

Skydancer stumbled along behind him, hitting most of the obstacles the other man skirted. He was not moving quietly, but even over the noise of his panting and the crunch of his feet clumsily snapping twigs, Red Hawk heard something. He stopped abruptly.

Skydancer was grimly plowing ahead, watching only the ground with his head down. He bumped heavily into Red Hawk's back. The alert Indian lost his balance, slipped on an icy patch of snow, but managed to keep from falling. He turned quickly, waving the gun. "Goddamn you! Can't you watch where the hell you're going?"

Skydancer grinned ruefully and shrugged his shoulders. "Sorry."

Red Hawk ignored him, head cocked to one side, listening for something in the trees around them.

Skydancer looked over his shoulder, eyeing the dark trees around them. "Why did we stop?"

Red Hawk motioned him to silence with a sharp hand gesture. Skydancer strained to hear but his city-dulled senses brought no sound beyond the wind. Yet he heeded the more experienced man and kept quiet. Red Hawk remained motionless, as if tracing the progress of something unseen with his ears. Finally, Skydancer could stand the suspense no longer. "What is it? Is it the cougar?" he asked, eyes darting about warily.

"Shut up!" snapped Red Hawk, straining to hear.

Skydancer stepped back, looking for a place of safety should the cougar spring upon them from the brush. Then he too could hear it. It was a drone, a faraway whine that seemed to be getting closer. It came from above. Skydancer beamed with newfound hope. It was the sound of a plane overhead just on the other side of the trees. He was saved!

"My God! It's a plane! Oh my God!" Skydancer dropped his case in his excitement, head back, arms waving up at the hole in the trees where the plane would pass over them.

Red Hawk pulled the .45 out of his belt and waved it at Skydancer. "I said shut up!"

But Skydancer did not hear him in his excitement over the possibility of being taken off the mountain. He shoved past Red Hawk toward a spot where a bright patch of sunlight shone down through the break in the leafy ceiling above them. "Jesus Christ! They're here!"

Skydancer limped to the center of the clearing. "I'm saved." He waved his arms. "Here I am!"

Red Hawk raised his .45 and pointed it at the center of Skydancer's back. "But I already saved you, fool," he said softly. Then louder over the building engine noise. "And first come, first served, I always say." He thumbed back the hammer of the .45.

Skydancer still did not hear him as he rushed headlong toward the center of the clearing. Red Hawk took careful aim and yelled, "Skydancer!"

Skydancer, his arms signaling wildly, turned at the sound of Red Hawk's voice. He stared unbelievingly at the gun.

"You take one more step and you die right where you are," Red Hawk said calmly. "Now turn around and walk back to me."

Skydancer shook his head in disbelief. "But the plane . . ." he began.

"Move!"

"But . . ."

"You're as much use to me dead as alive. Move!" Red Hawk snarled, the gun barrel steadily held on Skydancer.

Reluctantly, his eyes glancing back at the clearing, Skydancer stumbled forward, moving out of the clearing toward Red Hawk. The sound of the plane grew louder and it was this that threw Skydancer into a panic. "For Christ's sake, that's a plane up there! They're looking for me! Don't you hear it?"

Red Hawk beckoned with his gun, "All the way back to me. Just move quietly now, I mean it."

The sound of the plane filled the trees, shaking them. The two men stood facing each other, locked in silence as it passed almost directly overhead. Skydancer trembled and his whole body shook. So close! So goddamned close. Then the airplane was gone, the noise fading away to the south. "Now come all the way back. Get in front of me where you won't get into trouble." Red Hawk brandished the gun. "And don't make any sudden or unnecessary moves either, hear? I'd just as soon shoot you as look at you."

"You're insane," said Skydancer. "Why don't you let me go? You can't hold me prisoner. I haven't done anything to you."

For an answer, Red Hawk swung the pistol and connected solidly with the side of Skydancer's head. Skydancer slammed to the ground, stunned by the force of the blow. A new cut on the side of his head opened. Skydancer lay beside the briefcase he had abandoned in his excitement over the plane. He lifted his head and stared at Red Hawk.

"Why'd you do that?" asked Skydancer.

Red Hawk laughed. " 'Cause you're acting like a crazy white man. I bet you take your briefcase to bed with you too, don't you? Maybe I did it because I felt like it."

Skydancer looked down at his briefcase. His mind for the first time seemed crystal clear, as if the blow to the head had made him know who he was, as if it had awoken him from a long sleep.

Skydancer stood up slowly and then suddenly heaved the briefcase into the brush with a sideways snap of his wrists. It tumbled down a ravine, irretrievably lost.

It took Red Hawk by surprise.

"Why the hell did you do that?"

Skydancer shrugged. " 'Cause maybe you were right. I have been acting like a crazy white man. I may not know always how to act like an Indian, I may not seem Indian to you, but I'm just beginning to realize I'm Indian to myself."

With that, Skydancer closed his eyes and sank to the ground.

"You're going to be a dead Indian if you don't get up," said Red Hawk.

"Leave me alone."

Red Hawk prodded him with the toe of his boot.

Skydancer did not respond.

Angry, Red Hawk gave him a vicious kick. Skydancer responded to that. His eyes opened and he gasped with pain.

"Get up or I'll pistol-whip the crap out of you."

Slowly, painfully, Skydancer forced himself to stand. He'd been hurt enough. He didn't want any more pain.

"Okay, city Indian, you just walk on ahead of me and don't give me any trouble or I'll take your head off. I'll tell you which way to go." He motioned with the pistol to point the way. "Let's go find us an airplane."

The pilot of the Cessna 150 looked down as he cleared the ridge. A flash of black appeared for an instant against a white patch of snow. He banked the plane and circled once. Seeing nothing, he keyed the microphone.

"Rescue command, this is one-niner-tango-delta."

"We read you. Go one-niner," crackled the speaker.

"Completing sweep of grid fourteen. Thought I saw something moving but must have been some big animal or something. Area clear on my sweep. All clear, I repeat. I'm low on fuel. I'm coming in."

"Ah roger, one-niner, grid fourteen crossed off. Bring her home. The coffee's on."

The pilot nodded, taking one last look at the mountainside below him. He could think of no more inhospitable place to bring down a plane. "I pity the poor bastards if they came down up here somewhere," he said to himself, then he nosed his aircraft over and headed for the barn.

The black cougar listened to the sound of the engine recede in the distance, then it emerged from the thick brush to continue its journey. It moved in a straight path beside the clear track of human footprints in the snow, the recent mark of two men.

Prodded by Red Hawk, Skydancer led the way down a hillside, more falling than walking. Red Hawk followed, holding the pistol at the ready. At the bottom of the hill he was forced to stop and get his breath. Red Hawk sneered at the weakness of his captive and motioned him on with the gun toward a tall stand of trees near the lip of a gorge. "Move it, city boy. These tracks of yours aren't going to be here forever." Red Hawk eyed the erratic trail that had marked Skydancer's flight from the site of the crash. "Christ! I've seen gooks with broken legs who could walk straighter than you did. You must have been out of your goddamn mind."

"I don't know why you're doing this," said Skydancer, moving ahead wearily. He was almost at the end of his strength. "I don't know why you wouldn't let me contact that plane. I . . . I could have been rescued."

"Told you before. I don't need any help. And you've already been rescued. Now shut up and keep moving."

"Look," pleaded Skydancer. "There's no need for the gun. I couldn't hurt you if I wanted to."

"Have to keep it handy anyway. I'm not exactly afraid you'll decide to get brave." He pointed straight ahead. "That black bastard is out there somewhere. Okay, bear right, then straight. We got a good set of your tracks here." The new snow had not built up under the stand of trees and Skydancer's earlier footprints were clearly visible.

Skydancer followed directions but kept talking. "At least you could tell me what this is all about. Why are we trying to find the crash? They're all dead. I realize it's important the plane be found, but like I said, I've really got to get to Denver."

Red Hawk smiled. "How much cash you have on you when you left Frisco?"

"Like I said, I lost my billfold. I really don't know." Hope suddenly leaped to Skydancer's face. "But I'd gladly pay you to take me out of here. I'll write you a check. I've got some money in the bank."

That got Red Hawk's attention.

"How much money?"

"Close to a thousand. You can have it all. Just get me out of here."

Red Hawk grunted. "Chicken feed. How much you have on you in the plane?"

Skydancer was puzzled. "Hundred and a half, maybe two hundred."

Red Hawk laughed. "I ain't no mathematician, but you multiply that by the number of people on that plane and it comes to a nice piece of change. And that ain't even counting the jewelry and such."

Skydancer stopped dead in his tracks. He turned and confronted the man with the gun. His face betrayed his amazement. His eyes widened in disbelief. "You're not going to rob . . ." he said incredulously. "You're not going to rob . . . the . . . bodies . . ."

Red Hawk spat on the ground before replying. "Hell, yes. Ain't nobody gonna find that wreck on this mountain, at least not for one hell of a long time. 'Sides, nothing's wrong with taking what's not ever gonna do the original owners no good. Pick up your feet, keep moving." Red Hawk nudged him with the barrel of the .45.

Skydancer summoned whatever remnant of strength he had and stood his ground. The two men stared at each other. "And if I don't?"

"Then I'll just kill you right here, city boy Indian," said Red Hawk.

Skydancer moved.

27

The rented Cadillac followed the two-lane road through the foothills. Skyler Tannerman drove, watching for road signs as he maneuvered through the winding mountain curves.

Pamela sat in the back seat, her head resting against the shoulder of Michael. Michael was holding a tennis magazine with one hand and squeezing a rubber ball with his other hand, improving his tennis grip. He was a tennis pro who worked out of the North Moor Country Club.

He had an athlete's seasoned body and the mind of a tennis ball.

Skyler glanced at her in the rearview mirror, then brought his gaze back to the frosted windshield.

The heater hummed and even the steady stream of warmth that swirled out of the vents could not keep the mountain cold out.

"It's damn cold at this elevation," said Skyler, just making conversation. They had hardly spoken a word since the trip had started.

Pamela changed her position in the seat. She said nothing.

"Should be there soon if that yokel back at the gas station gave us the right directions."

Skyler looked at Pamela in the mirror again. She acted like he had never spoken.

"What did they tell you when you called?" A direct question would be difficult for her to duck.

"They said if the snow lets up they'd put the planes back into the air. They haven't found a trace of anything, so they sent out ground units this morning."

Skyler looked through the car window at the steep mountain as the car wound farther up the road. "Pretty rugged country."

Finally she spoke.

"I think I'm going to get married again, Father."

"Oh." He kept his eyes on the road.

"Marriage suits me. Don't you think so, Father. And think of the tax advantages."

"Really, Pamela, you're too much," said her father, gripping the wheel tightly.

"As soon as we find the body, as soon as we have proof positive that Skydancer is dead, Michael and I are going to be married. Are you happy for us, Father?" She smiled wickedly.

"What?" He didn't believe her. It was just her warped sense of humor, manifesting itself in the worst possible way.

Michael looked up from his magazine. He turned to Skyler. "You sure got a beautiful daughter, Mr. Tannerman. I sure would like to marry her, sir. Yes, I sure would."

"Shut up, Michael," said Pamela.

"Why don't you both shut up," said Skyler, who was tired of everyone and everything.

"But I'm serious, Father. Michael and I are going to be married. I may sound like I'm kidding but I'm quite serious." Her voice was as cold as the mountain air.

"But why? Why him, for Christ's sake? Couldn't you find anybody stupider?"

"Hey," said Michael feeling insulted.

"But that's why he's so perfect, Father. He's good in bed and a disaster every place else. He isn't bright enough to marry me for my money and he's too stupid to impose on you. The perfect son-in-law. You'll never see him. I'll keep him on a leash and only take him outside for walks."

"Hey," said Michael, his face red. "You shouldn't tease me so much already." He was so embarrassed he dropped his rubber ball and had to bend over and rummage around on the floor of the car, looking for it.

"Nothing would surprise me anymore," said Skyler. "And furthermore, I don't care what you do from now on. You're on your own. How long do you think you'll want to stay up here? I mean there's a chance they may never . . . What I'm trying to say is, it may take weeks."

"So I've got weeks. Too bad you don't, Father. Without those papers, you're really sweating bullets, aren't you?"

"I got a two-day extension and that's it," said Skyler. "And then the you know what hits the rotating blade."

Skyler spotted the outskirts of Northpass approaching.

The car pulled into the lot of a ramshackle motor court.

"The two of you get out here," said Skyler. "Two's company, but not in this case, if you ask me. Three is a positive disaster. I've got another hotel, just across town. I hope you enjoy being here as much as I enjoy not being here."

"Isn't my father a real sweetheart, Michael?" asked Pamela as she got out of the car.

Michael nodded, not sure if he should answer or not. He unloaded the luggage. Skyler drove off, leaving them standing there by their luggage. Her father hadn't even said goodbye.

Pamela saw the peeling paint, the unshielded light bulbs above the doors, and shook her head. This hotel was a real toilet.

Michael disappeared into the manager's office. Pamela stared at the mountain peaks, thrusting up into the slate-gray sky. She was bored and depressed, and despite her manner, even lonely. Tonight she was going to get drunk, really goddamn drunk.

Michael came out waving a key on a bright oblong of blue plastic. "I got it. This way." He motioned toward the back of the building and hefted the bags.

The room had a stuffed pheasant mounted on one wall, its faded colors a contrast with the aged knotty-pine paneling. There was one bed, a double, covered by a white chenille bedspread that was so yellowed and stained it looked like a topographical map. A nightstand and a mismatched dresser were the only other furnishings.

Pamela opened the drawer in the nightstand and peered in.

"Son of a bitch. Not even a Bible. Well, the hell with it. Unpack the booze."

"Ain't it kind of early to drink?" said Michael, frowning. "I mean, it ain't even ten in the morning yet."

"You're right. Sex first, then the booze. C'mere and help me tear off my clothes."

He moved to help her do just that.

As he ripped off her blouse, a hundred miles away Skydancer scrambled up a slight grade on the other side of a ravine. He fell to his knees breathlessly at the top. He looked down at the floor of the gorge some fifty yards below.

Red Hawk came up behind him, standing over him.

"Hot damn!" said Red Hawk, excited. "There it is!"

From their high vantage point they could see the wreck clearly. Foliage blocked most of the wreckage on the far side of the barrier but directly below they could see the tumbled heap that had been a 727. There was no movement in the wreckage.

Skydancer saw very clearly the body of a small child lying like a broken doll in the snow. "Oh God! Those poor people! Such a waste! My God!" He tried to control himself but he could not hold it in.

He began to cry, gently at first, then he gave in to it and sobbed unashamedly. Red Hawk gestured at the gorge. "Save it! Ain't doing them no good." Red Hawk nudged him with a boot. "Move on down there. We got work to do."

The cat covered the ground in giant leaps, flashing through the trees like an ebony lightning bolt, its heavy breathing filling the woods. Coming into a clearing, it skidded to a sudden stop, its nostrils flared. It walked slowly to a bush and nosed at something that lay half concealed in the leaves. Pushing with a massive paw, it forced Skydancer's briefcase out into the light.

It looked at the case, sniffing. Then, with an almost human gesture of disdain, it raked its claws over the black leather, ripping it as it cast it to one side. It growled, then loped out of the clearing into the trees.

Skydancer sat on a fallen tree trunk staring at a mass of twisted steel. The sun had passed overhead and long shadows filled the deep gorge. Red Hawk scavenged fifty feet away near the dam of fallen rocks that separated the gorge into two sections. He moved in a large circle as he worked.

Skydancer just sat and watched him.

From his perch he could see a noticeable lack of bodies and very little luggage. What suitcases were there were badly scorched and he could see from Red Hawk's expression that the looter was having very little luck.

Red Hawk kicked a piece of metal out of his way and turned to Skydancer. "This is only the forward section of the plane." He pointed to the other end of the gorge. "Must've come in that way. Looks like it exploded before it hit. Probably what threw you clear."

The running dialogue seemed distant to Skydancer, as if it came down a long tunnel. He shook his head to clear it.

"Nothing much of any value here," continued Red Hawk. He walked back to Skydancer. "I'm gonna have a look up the gorge behind them boulders . . ." He gestured in the direction Skydancer was facing, then he brought the gun back and centered it on Skydancer's forehead. Skydancer stiffened.

Red Hawk took careful aim and pulled back the hammer. Skydancer began to shake, wobbling on the log. "Please . . . I'll do anything you say . . . Don't shoot . . ."

Red Hawk pulled the trigger.

The hammer fell with a sharp metallic *click*. Skydancer stared up at him, hands flung up to protect his face, the awareness of death large in his eyes.

Red Hawk said, "That's what you'll get if you move." He pulled the slide back, injecting the shell into the chamber. "You stay put if you know what's good for you. Nowhere to run, so I won't tie you up, but you get to shouting at airplanes again, I'll shut you up for good."

Skydancer believed him. He sat trembling on the log.

He nodded, quick spasmodic jerks of his head. Red Hawk turned and started up the gorge. Skydancer watched him go, then vomited into the clean snow.

After the seizure had passed he sat for a long time. He was tired and he stared at the ground, unmoving. On the verge of sleep, he perched on the rough bark, leaning first one way and then the other, trying to keep awake. Rubbing his eyes, he looked up.

Right into the face of the black cougar.

28

The ground search units, made up of airmen, forest rangers and civilian volunteers, spread out into the mountains. Three groups of a dozen men on horseback, bundled against the cold, picked their way through the melting snow as they ascended into the higher elevations. They led pack animals laden with radio equipment and supplies through wide meadows that fronted the towering range.

Group C, led jointly by Frank Scanlon and Lloyd Fiske, pointed its mounts due north on a line of sight with the last known position of the lost aircraft. By 3 P.M. the ground temperature had risen to fifty-six degrees. Fiske unzipped his heavy parka and relaxed in the saddle. He looked at Scanlon beside him and then at the unrelenting mountains ahead.

"You go 'head and lead in, Lloyd. I'll hang back a little so I can keep an eye on these Sunday-morning mountaineers," quipped Scanlon as he drew his reins back. Fiske nodded, turning his horse through a shallow stream. He nudged the animal on, with the highest peak in the distance his target.

He didn't know it yet but he was on a collision course with the remains of flight 193.

Back at the command trailer, an obviously refreshed Skyler Tannerman, wearing an expensively tailored suit, entered and looked around for someone in charge. An aide directed him to Colonel Tucker. The ragged Air Force officer was a man walking in his sleep. The dark circles under his eyes gave him a haunted appearance.

Skyler walked to his makeshift desk, a few two-by-fours spread across two sawhorses. He moved and stood over the officer until the colonel was finally forced to look up and acknowledge his presence. "Yes," he said shortly.

"Excuse me, Colonel. I'm Skyler Tannerman. I'm the father of the wife of one of the passengers aboard the plane. She's quite concerned and I thought I'd check with you to see what progress has been made."

Tucker gestured obliquely and went back to the papers on his desk. "There's an FAA man and an airline rep staggering around here somewhere. They're handling all public relations inquiries." It was a dismissal but Skyler did not move.

"There is more to this than just a personal loss, Colonel. That's why I came directly to you," Skyler said firmly.

The colonel sighed and looked up, appraising the determined man that stood before him. "I'm afraid I can't tell you anything more than they could. And I really don't have the time to console hysterical . . . ah, concerned relatives."

"The man in question was my employee. He was carrying valuable documents of incalculable worth. They cannot be replaced. Barring anything else, those papers must be found at all costs. Tell me, Colonel, in all candor, what are the chances of anybody coming out of those mountains alive."

Tucker leaned back in his chair and scratched his head. "On a scale of one to ten? A minus five."

"I see."

Tucker watched Skyler shift uncomfortably from one foot to the other. A tinge of regret struck him for being so brusque with somebody who just wanted a little information. He decided to make amends. "Like a cup of coffee? It's miserable but it's the best I can offer."

Skyler shook his head. "Thanks anyway . . . Are you going to continue the air search?"

"Yeah, we just got a weather clearance. Should have the birds back in the air within the hour . . . not that I expect much. That country's the worst I've ever seen." Tucker was anxious to talk now, hoping he had not offended the serious man before him with his curt manner. "We have three ground units out too and when we get anything definitive I'll let you know. You at a motel?"

Skyler nodded. "Yes, I'm at the Vagabond Motor Court." He hesitated and then he said, "My daughter is at the Silver Rainbow

Hotel. Rooms 112 and 113. You can reach us there, at least for the next couple of days."

Tucker sipped his coffee, watching Skyler over the rim of the cup. "Then I'll call you, or Mrs. . . . ?"

"Skydancer. Mrs. John Skydancer."

"You or Mrs. Skydancer the minute we have any news."

Skyler nodded his thanks and turned on his heel. The colonel watched him go, then shook his head.

The black image had an out-of-focus quality as Skydancer rubbed his eyes and shook his head. The cat was moving down the hillside toward him, very slowly, watching him with a fixed gaze. The long body moved liquidly over the ground but the eyes stayed on Skydancer, gauging him.

Skydancer tried to shout but no sound came from his cracked lips. He sat rooted in terror as the animal approached. The cat stopped twenty feet from the log before it took its eyes from the shaking man. It looked at the ground. Skydancer watched as it lowered its head and began to circle the log, studying the tracked snow. He shivered with fear and made a move to slide back along the fallen tree. The giant head snapped up and the cat growled. Skydancer froze.

The cat found a boot print in the snow and sniffed it. Skydancer scrunched back as it snarled again and looked in the direction Red Hawk had taken. Then it let out a terrifying roar and loped off up the gorge. Skydancer fell backwards off the log and landed on his side in the snow, trembling.

Behind the boulders that bisected the gorge was a scene of carnage. The 727 passenger compartment was embedded in the snow and rocks, almost intact. A jagged rip split the hull down its full length. Bodies were spread out around it.

Red Hawk stood looking down at the destruction. He studied the corpses thrown haphazardly among the boulders and bushes, caught in burned and twisted metal, lifeless dolls strewn about by a careless giant.

He moved into the center of the debris and stopped. Directly in front of him sat the body of a man braced upright in the rocks, facing him. It stared with open eyes at the intruder. Red Hawk leaned down and patted the man's pockets, avoiding the blank stare. He removed a wallet from what was left of the corpse's suit coat. Opening it, he quickly counted out the bills and stuffed them into one of the side pockets of his heavy jacket.

Kneeling, he removed a watch from a stiff wrist and twisted a ring from one of the fingers. As he leaned forward to check the trouser pockets he jumped back, startled. The corpse was legless. Rising, he wiped his hands on his coat and moved on.

He darted here and there like a hungry bee, lifting the icy arm of a woman to get at her brooch, turning over a man to get into his pockets. His eyes gleamed and his breathing became hard and fast. His hands were full of bloodstained booty and his jacket pockets bulged.

He looked around, spotting a large flat rock at knee level. Going to it, he placed his loot on the ground and removed his coat. He spread the coat open over the rock. He reached to the ground, scooped up the money and jewelry, dropping the pile into the center of the coat. He smiled as he moved back into the wreckage.

Half an hour later the pile of valuables had grown substantially larger. He foraged back and forth between the bodies and the rock, his busy hands adding more wealth to the pile.

High in the boulders behind him the cat sat, still, watching like a black statue. Only its eyes followed the movements of the scavenger below.

Red Hawk dragged a heavy piece of luggage to the rock. He tugged on the handle but the bag was locked. He swore as he pulled the .45 from his waist. He fired one shot that took the lock off the bag, handle and all.

The sound of the shot did not seem to disturb the cat. It sat, waiting.

The bag fell open to reveal women's clothing, nylon hose, frilly underwear and a leather box. Red Hawk set the gun down on the rock. He broke open the box, emptying its contents over the pile. "Ooowee!" he exclaimed as a mass of silver and turquoise Indian jewelry dribbled through his fingers to mix with the other spoils.

The cat watched the silver reflect the sunlight. It did not move.

Red Hawk came away from the rock, shuffling through more luggage. The .45 remained on the rock. The cat stared at the gun and then slowly rose, creeping forward.

In the center of the wreckage Red Hawk searched for more loot, turning over sheets of metal, pushing corpses away with his heavy boots. He stopped to look down on a doll alone on a patch of snow. Kicking it out of his way, he turned to face a complete seat, still occupied by three bodies and half buried in a drift. Digging in the loose snow around the seat, he quickly removed anything of value he could find.

Turning past the seat, he was confronted by a standing man.

A piece of jagged steel speared the man through the back, holding him upright. Red Hawk searched him and went on.

What was once an elderly lady sat crushed against the back of a seat. The top half of the seat was gone. The woman was headless. Around her neck a diamond pendant rested, miraculously intact. Red Hawk removed it gingerly, stuffing it into a shirt pocket as he moved farther away from the rock. And his gun.

"Excuse me, Mr. White Man. You wouldn't have change for a thousand by any chance?" he said as he removed a wallet from the inside coat pocket of another lifeless body. Dropping the wallet on the man's chest, he counted out the bills: "Six, seven, eight, eight fifty . . ."

The cat watched him sift the green paper through his fingers.

". . . nine, nine twenty-five . . . not quite a thousand, but that's okay," he said, smiling. He stuffed the wad of bills into his shirt and grabbed the man's hand, trying to remove a large ruby ring from a scorched finger. He tugged and pulled but the ring held fast. Taking his knife from the sheath at his side, he hacked away at the frozen hand until he had removed the ring, the finger with it.

His shirt pockets were full now and he turned back to the rock. A small croak of surprise issued from his throat as he looked at the booty-laden rock.

Stretched across the rock and nestled in the loot was the cat, its eyes smoldering with hatred.

His gun was inches from its right forepaw.

It growled and Red Hawk froze, the beads of perspiration on his forehead becoming ice drops. His hands fell to his sides and the bills fluttered to the ground from his lax fingers. He unsheathed his belt knife and stared at the cat.

The black cougar did not move. Red Hawk took a tentative step backward, feeling the rough ground with the heel of his boot. The cat growled again. Red Hawk stopped. He bent over very slowly and picked up a small rock. Straightening, he threw the rock at the cat. "Yiiiiiiiiii!" he yelled as the rock smashed just in front of the cat.

The cat did not move. Did not even flinch. Red Hawk's defiant cry had been tainted with fear. The cat seemed to recognize that.

In answer, the huge cougar adjusted its body on the rock, more a shifting of weight than preparation for attack. Its right foreleg brushed the gun and it fell off the rock. It landed in the snow in front of the cat, between the rock and Red Hawk. He looked at the gun longingly.

Without warning the cat rose and stepped down to stand over the gun. Then it flowed toward the man with the knife, a black blot on the snow.

Red Hawk panicked. He turned, lost his balance and recovered, breaking into a scrambling run. He jumped a piece of wreckage and went to his knees on the other side, gasping, the knife held tightly in one hand. He fought desperately for breath, then rose to his feet to stumble on. The cat cleared the charred metal in a graceful leap and landed behind him. It hissed, watching as he ran on.

Red Hawk flayed his way through the seats, falling and rising, his face and arms bleeding from the jagged aluminum and razor-sharp wires. The cat weaved silently through the debris, following at a steady pace. In terror Red Hawk looked back over his shoulder, forcing his strained limbs to move faster.

The cat moved easily behind him. Red Hawk was breaking and the cat knew it.

The Indian plunged on madly. His foot tangled in something and he went to the ground on top of a body. The dead man's eyes were open, staring into Red Hawk's face. He screamed and pulled away from the corpse, crawling on his knees. Incoherent mutterings tumbled from his throat. But Red Hawk did not drop the knife.

Looking up, he found his path blocked by the sloping side of the fuselage. He slid up the hull to a standing position, trying to scale the smooth metal. His fingernails scratched futilely at the hull and he fell back, again and again. Hearing a snarl behind him, he spun to face the cat, his back pressed to the cold steel.

The cat was three feet away, blocking any retreat he might have hoped for. The animal looked up at him, its long body angling away, its jaws working in a sideways grinding motion. All reason fell away from the frightened man. He began to talk to his tormentor. "I'm not gonna hurt you . . . I wouldn't hurt you now . . ."

Taking a few bills from his shirt, he waved them at the cat.

"See, all's I want is the money . . ." His voice quivered. "Jus' leave me be and I swear, I won't come after you again . . ."

His voice turned high and shrill as the cat moved closer. "I swear! I don't have no fight with you no more!" He waved his hand at the cat. The hand that held the knife. The cat looked at the knife and growled. Red Hawk looked blankly at the sharp blade in his hand. "What? The knife?" He gazed at it as if he were seeing it for the first time. "No, no." He shook his head. "I wouldn't use it . . . See?" He tossed the knife to one side. It hit the hull with a clang and bounced to the ground.

The cat watched it settle in the snow.

"See, I don't have it no more . . ." The cat edged closer. Red Hawk began to sob. "Please! I can't hurt you now. I don't have my guns." He spread his hands. "See?" Then he began to giggle uncontrollably. "You took my rifle . . ."

Red Hawk pointed over the cat's head in the direction of the rock wall that divided the gorge. "Please, there's another man over there. You go get him. You'll like *him* . . ." His thoughts focused on Skydancer as he fought to clear his head. He raised his voice and shouted, "Skydancer! For God's sake, help me!" The sound of his voice was lost in the wreckage.

The cat hissed and began to move its head back and forth. Its tail stiffened. Red Hawk cringed back against the hull. "No, no . . . noooo!"

The cat lifted from the ground, a smooth upward movement of its forequarters. It towered over the trembling man for an instant. Then it came down. Red Hawk screamed as its claws hooked into his shoulder blades, ripping downward.

Securing the convulsive figure against the hull, it brought a foot up, claws extended, and tore at Red Hawk's torso, eviscerating him.

As Red Hawk's scream became a terrible, high-pitched wail, the cat cocked its head to one side and closed its gaping jaws over his face. And the scream died as Red Hawk died.

29

Solomon stared into the depths of the fire. Lianna shoved another log into the fire, stirred up the ashes. Suddenly, she clutched her chest as if in pain and staggered, almost falling.

The old man leapt out of his chair. He got his arms around her before she fell. She jerked convulsively, almost tearing herself out of his grasp.

"Lianna! Lianna, what's wrong?"

A convulsion wracked her frail old body. Her eyes bulged and she threw back her head, screaming.

Solomon put his arms around her tightly, cradling her to his chest. He had seen this thing in her only once before. Just once, and that had been when their first child, only four years old, had fallen off a cliff and died.

The spasms passed, leaving her weak, drained.

"Lianna. What's wrong?" asked Solomon again, already suspecting.

"He's dead," said the old woman, her voice almost a whisper. "The mountain has claimed him."

He helped her to her chair. "It had to come," he said.

The old woman was crying.

The old man left her crying softly in her chair and went over to look out the open door at the mountain. It rose above the cabin like an eagle about to swoop on its prey. The mountain had not changed. It had the power to kill and the power to heal. It was fashioned out of great mystery and it was now as it had been since the mountain first rose into the sky, great and awesome.

The old man went outside. He went to his knees, eyes fixed on the mountain. He lifted his hands and held them out to the mountain.

"I thank you, Spirit House. I thank you for giving my son a good death."

Tears, unbidden, fell down his wrinkled cheeks.

"A good death."

A chill wind blew down off the mountain, striking the old man suddenly. The old man gasped, as if his heart had touched ice.

Something brushed against his cheek, borne on the wind. It fell in front of him.

He picked it up. It was much too heavy to have been carried by the cold breeze that had deposited it at his feet. Much too heavy.

It was a thick clump of jet-black hair, stained brown with dried blood.

It was Red Hawk's.

30

Skydancer was running. As soon as the madman with the gun had gotten out of sight, Skydancer had fled. He did not think Red Hawk would abandon the rich harvest of loot just to pursue him.

His long coat, open to the wind, flowed behind him like a cape as he bolted over the rough ground. The branches of trees attacked his face and arms. His frenzied flight carried him through the forest.

Reaching a hillside, he fell, scraping his knees on the jagged rocks. He rose, groaning, and fled into the night. At an ankle-deep stream he slowed, splashed through and collapsed on the far bank, his feet still in the water. He pulled himself painfully around to face the brook. Panting, he dipped a hand into the chilled water.

He rubbed the coldness on his filthy face and his breathing subsided from uncontrolled gasps to measured spasms. Cupping a hand to his lips, he licked at his damp fingers. As he went back to drink again, something moved. A small shape scuttled out of the water beside him and he screamed.

Jumping back, he fell into a bush, rolled over in the foliage and scampered to his feet, well back from the stream. He ran blindly into the darkness.

A full moon bathed him as he crawled through the thick brush. No sound could be heard over his labored breathing. He constantly looked back over his shoulder, eyes wide with fear, hoping to keep what was out there at a distance. Leaning his head against the bole of a tree, he stopped to get his bearings.

He pressed his cheek to the rough bark, using the stinging pain to pull him out of his exhaustion. Inwardly, he hoped for a reprieve.

He calmed down. As his heaving chest took on more normal constrictions, an owl hooted, no more than a foot above his head.

He went into the air as if someone had set his clothing ablaze. When he came down he was running again, crashing through the trees.

He went to ground a half mile away, wracked by a fit of coughing. Beside him was a burned-out husk of what was once a large tree. The tree had been struck by lightning long ago and the resulting fire had gouged out its center, leaving it a topless stump as high as his chest. He saw the blackened, three-sided shelter and pulled himself through the narrow gap to the inside of the stump.

Shivering more from fright than the night chill, he tucked the remains of his topcoat around him and huddled back as far as he could go, his eyes glued to the opening in front of him. He fought to stay awake but sleep overcame him almost instantaneously.

His dreams were episodic. Pleasant thoughts of Pamela merged with the giant black face of the cat trying to lock its fangs into his groin. The nightmare tortured him; fighting off the cat and reaching out for his wife drained him completely. Soon he was not able to differentiate between the two.

Twenty miles to the south, Lloyd Fiske stirred a pot over a campfire. Sleeping bags and pup tents lined the clearing in which group C had made camp for the night. Scanlon toyed with a radio unit, trying to contact base. He supervised the fresh-faced youth in fatigues and parka as he rigged up a transmitter powerful enough to be used in these high mountains.

Fiske tasted the stew and called out, "Ain't no way you're gonna raise base 'til we get out of this valley. I don't care how good your set is. Anyway, soup's on."

Scanlon nodded to the boy, who switched off the radio, then he joined Fiske at the fire. The other men tending the horses followed suit and soon dinner was being served all around. Fiske ate slowly, spooning the hot gravy into his mouth with a piece of bread. He watched the night sky as he savored the warmth in his mouth. The moon was beginning to disappear behind a bank of heavy clouds. Scanlon put down his plate and nodded at Fiske, then jerked his head skyward. "What do you think?"

Fiske continued to study the clouds that were beginning to resemble the mountains they flowed over. "I think it's gonna snow again. When we're through we ought to see that these kids are tucked in safely for the night. Then maybe, you and me, we can play a little blackjack."

Scanlon smiled. "You still hustling nickels and dimes from the tourists with that marked deck of yours?"

"I'd take offense at that"—Fiske scowled, then grinned widely —"if it weren't true." He reached into his pocket and removed a deck of cards, held them up to an ear and flipped through them.

"Then why eliminate these guys? They probably all have a few bucks in their jeans."

"Yeah, well, they look pretty bushed to me. Besides, we ought to be up and out of here come sunup."

"Maybe we'll luck out and one of the other groups will spot the plane. Then I can go home to the loving wife and you can go back to busting drunks."

Fiske thought of Red Hawk, then dismissed him from his mind.

He shuffled the cards slowly, looking across the fire at Scanlon. "There's more to this job than roustin' an occasional D and D, Frank. Why, I remember once I had to single-handedly subdue a felon in the midst of an armed robbery."

"You arrived on the scene that fast, huh?"

"Well, way it was, he was tryin' to get back the money I won from him at cards."

Scanlon shook his head and said, "Lloyd?"

"Yeah?"

"Shut up and deal."

The snow came later, little flakes of iridescence that shimmered in the light from the still burning campfire. Fiske opened his eyes as the first snowflakes touched his face. Looking skyward from the folds of his mummy bag, he nodded. "Yep."

Dawn brought a clear sky and bright sun. Group C broke camp and rode out along a snow-covered spur that overlooked a sheer cliff. Scanlon was in the lead as they moved carefully, single file, over the narrow trail.

The new snowpack made the going difficult. Fiske rode behind the ranger, forced to squaw-rein his mount to the left to keep its head into the cliff. Scanlon led easily, the leather thongs held lightly between two fingers, left hand in his mackinaw pocket.

Fiske saw it coming but he could do nothing but rein in and shout at his friend. "Look out, Frank! She's goin'!"

Scanlon turned to look back and the forelegs of his horse collapsed as the bank broke away. He screamed as he tried to jump for the inside wall but it was too late. He went over with the horse, jackknifing down the side of the cliff to the boulder-strewn gorge below.

Fiske quickly dismounted, shouting commands to the shocked men behind him. Horses were led back and a rope slapped into Fiske's outstretched hand. He made it fast on an outcropping and, not waiting for help, tore off his parka and began to descend. He flipped himself out from the face of the cliff, the rope burning his gloves, feet striking the slippery granite as he slid down.

"Get on that goddamn radio and tell them we need a helicopter here with a medic aboard! Now!" he shouted as he reached the man in the gorge.

Scanlon groaned as he tried to turn over on his side. His right arm was twisted grotesquely under his chest and there was a deep gash in his leg. The snow was red around his ankle.

"Easy," Fiske said, trying to make the man comfortable. "Don't move 'til I can stop that bleeding."

"Oh, shit, I think I broke my goddamn arm!" moaned Scanlon.

"I don't doubt it, you clumsy bastard." Fiske tied off a tourniquet around Scanlon's thigh and pulled the man's arm out from under him. Scanlon's face went ashen from the pain but he managed to speak.

"How's my horse?"

"Dead. Broke its fool neck. Now shut up and lay still." Fiske looked up to the milling men above him. "Well?"

"There's a chopper just north of us on patrol!" shouted the radio operator. "It'll be here in ten minutes!"

"Well, don't just stand there gawkin' like a bunch of idiots! Rig a block and tackle and a blanket stretcher. The rest of you go find someplace for the chopper to land! There's a spot about three hundred yards back along the cut that should be big enough! Mark it with a flare!"

He looked back at Scanlon. "We'll have you out of here in a few minutes. Just relax."

Scanlon grimaced in pain. "Looks like you got the duty now, ole buddy."

"You horse's rear end! You probably planned it this way so I couldn't win my money back."

"Yeah, I rode off a cliff just to save six lousy bucks. I . . . ." He passed out.

Fiske looked up at the sky, watching for any sign of the helicopter. As he did, Skydancer tossed in his cramped sleep and pulled his arms across his chest.

He pressed into the hard wood, trying to get away from the dampness that was all around him. Suddenly, his eyes snapped open. He did not know where he was. The snow had piled at the entrance of the stump, obscuring his view of the woods. His coat was covered and he began to shake it off as if it were a contagious disease.

Birds sang in the branches overhead. Above their melodious chirping a whirling sound permeated the air. Freeing himself of the encumbering snow, he dug frantically at the entrance of the stump. The soft whirling sound grew louder.

On his feet, he stumbled out of the safety of the dead tree, a man alone, battered and near his breaking point. Away from the stump the sound was louder. He heard it and looked up. Above him the pines waved loosely in the breeze, blocking his view of the sky. As the noise came directly overhead he finally realized what it was.

He hoisted his ragged coat high and began to run. A hundred yards ahead a sun-drenched clearing broke the continuity of the woods. To this he sprinted, his legs pumping, his hands holding the folds of the coat high, like a matron running for a bus.

He was on the verge of a coronary when he reached the clearing. The helicopter had reached it several seconds before and now it was just in sight through a space in the trees. Skydancer raised his arms and shouted, "Over here! I'm here! Stop! . . . Come back!"

He ran around the clearing waving madly at the sky. "Damnit! I'm down here! Can't you see me?"

On his last word the copter stopped in the sky and hovered. Skydancer was almost felled by the relief that surged through his beaten body. "Thank you, thank you."

He smiled and looked up. The copter hung stationary in the sky for several seconds, then banked left and moved off. He shook his head from side to side, as if a bone had lodged in his throat. The copter gained speed toward the south and was soon out of sight. Its sound lasted a few moments longer, then blended with the wind.

Skydancer's eyes glazed and he sat down suddenly in the snow.

31

By noon the next day Frank Scanlon was resting comfortably in a Denver hospital, one arm in a cast. He told outrageous lies about his injuries to anyone who would listen.

Back on the mountain called Spirit House, a tired Fiske stood beside his horse eating a sandwich and sipping coffee from a paper cup.

The ground temperature had risen to fifty-eight degrees and his parka was tied to the back of his saddle. He wore wire-rimmed sunglasses and he pushed them back on the bridge of his nose with his wrist as he took another bite of the sandwich.

Behind him, the rest of the group lounged near their horses, relaxing after the arduous climb of the last two hours. The radioman fidgeted with the set that was tied to the hindquarters of a pack-horse. Intermittent squawks of static pierced the tranquil mountainside.

Fiske took a last bite, followed it with a swig of coffee and walked to the set. "Anythin'?" he asked the youthful technician.

"Nope. We should be able to raise them again when we reach that rise." The radio operator pointed to a summit several hundred yards ahead. "I did pick up a transmission from Air Six about half an hour ago. They're covering this grid pretty thoroughly."

"And?" asked Fiske as he crushed the paper cup and flipped it aside. It landed in a bush. The radioman looked at it, scowling at the littering.

"They reported nothing unusual sighted. Figure they were talking to HQ, even though I only got one side of the transmission. If any other groups found anything, Air Six would have been on top of it instead of here. I'll confirm that when we regain contact again."

"You do that." Fiske walked back to his horse and swung into the saddle. He waved his arm as he nudged his mount with his knees. "Okay, let's get movin'."

Five miles since sunup wasn't bad, thought Fiske. He guessed they could do three more today if the weather held.

Skydancer had covered five and he looked it.

He knelt over a rivulet of melting snow and drank greedily. The icy-cold water numbed his lips. He rested there on his knees, exhausted, aches and pains all through his body. His topcoat was torn in many places. Long streamers of ripped material hung to the ground, giving Skydancer the appearance of wearing an animal skin. His face and arms were cut and bruised. He had dried blood in his hair and on the front of his coat. He looked like a man who had been through a cement mixer.

As he kneeled there beside the cold running stream he tried to remember back to the days of his childhood, to a time that was more in keeping with the wilderness he was now lost in. Back on the reservation he had been closer to nature, more in tune with the rules of survival. His people had had the knowledge to survive in mountains like these, in places even more inhospitable than this. But he could not seem to remember anything useful.

It had been all so very, very long ago and he had spent so many years putting it all behind him. He tried to remember some of the things the old people had tried to teach him. But their faces and words were a million miles away, a part of a life he had been glad to lose. Now he regretted that loss.

Perhaps if his father had not been a drunk who spent most of his time in jail, perhaps then there would have been things Skydancer would have learned, wilderness survival skills which were a basic part of his people's culture. But on the reservation the old ways flourished only in the shadow of the white man's world. That shadow had engulfed Skydancer's father and taken him from the world. Young Skydancer had tried to pass from the shadow into the light of the white man. Adopted and raised by white people, he spent all his years trying to make a place for himself as one of them in their world.

On his knees in the snow now, he wished he knew more about

the world he had abandoned. He was hungry, he was cold, every part of him ached. He knew he could not survive much longer outdoors. He needed shelter, food and a fire. He needed to know the way out and he needed new clothes, something warm to keep out the cold that bit mercilessly at his flesh.

Skydancer had a wild look about him as his eyes darted from side to side. The cougar was out there somewhere. Since he had escaped from Red Hawk, he had had an eerie feeling that he was watched, that something stalked him, that something terrible moved just beyond his sight in the trees around him.

He scrambled to his feet and staggered toward the tree. Falling to his knees at the base of the tree, he began to dig frantically around the bole of the tree. Scraping his fingers raw, he made sharp rasping sounds from the back of his throat as he dug. He just hoped he remembered right.

He had. His effort was rewarded, however, by only a single small object near the frozen dirt beneath the snow. It was a walnut. Tiny as it was, it represented food and he greedily pressed it to his mouth. Ten minutes of frantic digging uncovered no more nuts. His fingers felt like they had been sandpapered. He could dig no more. It was no use.

His mind cast about for some other means of digging and then he remembered something else from his childhood. Hadn't someone used forked sticks to rake the snow? Yes. He searched through the brush until he found a dead branch that would suit his purposes.

He raked the snow around the base of the tree and was rewarded for his efforts with almost a dozen nuts. He ate them all and they were like ambrosia to his shriveled stomach. He had eaten some bark the night before, or rather had tried to, and this morning he had found something soft and white under a decaying log. If he had been a little hungrier he could have brought himself to eat it but that morning he could not. Now he would have eaten it gladly.

Part of his mind shielded him from these thoughts as he gulped down the bitter fragments of nut. He crushed the last walnut and the echo of the blow seemed to come back to him from a rise two hundred yards away. Suddenly it made him aware of things in the forest around him. He stopped to listen. The mountain seemed to bring a strange echo back to him.

The sound came again, a rhythmic beating, not unlike someone hammering. The wind was blowing now but the tapping sound was loud over it. Rising, he limped out on the flat ground in the direction of the rise.

The noise gained in intensity as he neared the sloping top of the hill. He broke into a clumsy run on legs that had already come too far. "I'm here! I'm over here!" he shouted, the sound of his voice surprising him with its coarseness. The thought that the noise might have come from Red Hawk did not occur to him.

The noise seemed to be coming from just the other side of the rise and Skydancer fell again and again as he stumbled his way up the soft snow and mud to the top. "Please wait!" he screamed, clawing his way up the hill, forced to go on hands and knees at the very top. "Please wait . . . Here I am . . . I'm coming . . ."

He reached the top of the slope completely out of breath. Skydancer tumbled to his knees at the top and looked with hope down into the gorge below. The smile that had been forming on his lips died.

Below him was the wreckage of the 727. A loose sheet of aluminum still attached to the horizontal stabilizer moved in the breeze, banging against it. Skydancer stared wordlessly at the banging metal sheets as if they had betrayed him somehow. He realized he had been going in circles ever since he had escaped from Red Hawk. This was too much.

He knew he was going to die there. He knew it was only a matter of time, a few hours. He did not understand why he and he alone should survive the crash only to die of exposure on the mountain. His making it through the crash hardly seemed worth it.

Skydancer wondered where Red Hawk was. In a way he hoped he would find him again. It had occurred to him that Red Hawk would probably shoot him on sight and in a curious sort of way he was almost looking forward to it. It would be better than starving or freezing to death, or worse, dying under the claws of the big cougar he had seen.

Skydancer fell forward on his face, exhaustion claiming the last of his strength. He lay there, without hope, face down in the dirt.

And there was something that moved behind him, something that watched him with eyes that burned in the gloom of the forest.

32

Jason Schneider was seven years old and he did not know how to ski yet. He watched as his father, dressed in a bright orange jacket, sped down the slope and schussed into the depression near the road. The van was parked there, a yellow piece of plastic awning hung from its opened door.

The man waved at his son and the boy waved back. Then he began the steep climb back to the top of the hill, using his ski poles like crutches.

Jason was bored. He kicked at the snow and began to explore his surroundings. Off to one side the slope leveled off to end in a mound of snow with spring grass beginning to break through. To this he walked, being careful to keep the van in sight, as his parents had taught him on their many ski trips.

Sitting on top of the mound, he played with the tips of the grass, pulling them out and throwing the strands into the air. Then he began to build a snowman. It took shape gradually on the mound. As it grew, the boy had to move farther away to push the snow up on the mound.

On the other side of the hill he scooped deeply and hit something cold and hard. It was a hand.

He looked at it curiously, not really understanding what he had found. Digging deeper, he exposed the top of a head. Looking into the face of the corpse, he screamed. His father was halfway down the slope when he heard the boy's shrill yell. He turned and banked, a rooster tail of snow building in his wake. He was beside his son in a matter of seconds.

The man looked down at the grisly remains and pushed the boy toward the van. He removed his skis, planting them upright in the snow to mark the discovery.

The van was equipped with a citizens band radio. Schneider clicked it to the emergency channel and called for help. He picked up another CBer in Meeker, who got on a land line to the police. Forty-five minutes later an Air Force helicopter landed in the road beside the van.

Several hours later Abe Tucker sighed deeply and dialed the number of the motor court. He was connected to room 12 and Skyler answered. Tucker hesitated for a second, then said, "Colonel Tucker here. I think you better come over here right away. Alone."

The line clicked at the other end and he replaced the receiver carefully in the cradle. A junior officer hovered over him holding a hastily written press release in his hand. "Sir?"

Tucker waved him away. "Give it to Harper, the FAA man. He'll know what to do with it."

"Don't you want to check it first?"

"What I want is a good stiff drink. Now get that damn thing to Harper before that pack of reporters outside overturn this trailer."

Skyler fought his way through the people at the door and made his way to Tucker's desk. Tucker looked up and indicated a folding chair that leaned against one of the sawhorses. "Sit down."

Skyler unfolded the chair and sat.

"I'm afraid I have some bad news. A body was discovered earlier today about a hundred and twenty-five miles north of here. It was badly burned but identification was possible due to the personal effects that were found on the man." Tucker watched the expression on Skyler's face.

Skyler rested back in the chair, a look of relief mingled with resignation crossing his features. "Well, it wasn't unexpected, I guess. I'm just not really sure how my daughter will take it. However, as Senator Townsend called you . . . He did call, didn't he?"

Tucker nodded grimly.

"The important thing here is the recovery of the documents. I'm sure the senator was able to convey to you how vital it is that they be recovered."

"It wasn't the lady's husband."

"What? Then who . . . ?"

Tucker pushed a piece of paper across the desk. "It was the pilot of the 727."

Skyler looked at the paper, trying hard to focus on the typed info on the sheet. "It . . . it has three names here."

"A search of the immediate vicinity uncovered two more bodies. That of the flight engineer and what must be the remains of the copilot. We haven't got positive ID on the third body yet but what was left of the fingerprints was wired to Washington. We should have confirmation before dark."

"Did you find the plane?"

"No." He took the paper Skyler handed back.

"I don't understand."

"We searched a ten-mile radius around the bodies. There was no sign of anything else. The air crew was very badly burned. Our best guess is that there was a fire aboard, possibly caused by an explosion. The condition of the bodies suggests that they were forcibly ejected from the flight deck, and from a very high altitude."

Skyler leaned forward and placed both hands flat on the desk. "Look, am I supposed to decode this or are you going to give it to me straight? What are the chances of anybody coming out of this alive, or failing that, the documents surviving the crash, unburned and still legible?"

Tucker scratched the thinning hair on the back of his head and looked directly into Skyler's eyes. "The only thing I'd bet on at this point, Mr. Tannerman, is that the aircraft is no longer airborne."

It was the strength of the morning sun on his face that brought Skydancer awake finally. He was half frozen, lying in the brush on the little hill above the site of the crash. It was the sun too that had thawed him out, kept him from dying of exposure, of the cold of that high altitude. Skydancer was not thankful to be alive.

He moved his hands in front of his face, conscious of pain in his joints, pain in his arms and legs and back. Hunger tore at his insides like an angry animal. His lips were cracked and broken. He did not want to move at all, would not have moved if it had not been for the extreme discomfort of his present position.

Painfully he dragged himself down the hill, moving toward the wrecked plane. He had no purpose in mind; indeed, his mind was disorganized. He was very much on the edge and his thoughts were far from sane.

"I'm going to be late, don't you see?" he said as he stepped unsteadily through the wreckage. Reaching the far side of the fuselage, he braced his back against a rock and faced the body of a man. Skydancer's eyes were cloudy as he spoke to the corpse. "You see, I've got to get to Denver to get this contract signed." He paused, as if hearing a reply.

When he continued, his voice was lower, almost calm. "You don't understand. I swear to you, it's of the utmost importance. If I'm late, I'll lose everything, my job, my wife, my children I don't even know, my mortgage, my . . . my everything."

Skydancer turned his head. Was that Pamela's voice? Yes, it must be. It seemed to reverberate through his entire being. *"If you blow this one, don't come back!"* Skydancer shook his head and scrambled forward on his hands and knees. Grabbing the dead man by the shirtfront, he looked deep into its sightless eyes.

"Please help me." The corpse twisted and fell away from Skydancer's clutching hands. Skydancer stared down at the body. "Go on! Turn your back on me! Ignore me!" he raved. "I tell you, I *know* I can do it! I *can* get that contract!"

"Don't come back!" said Pamela.

Skydancer spun around and shouted at the sky. "Shut up, damn you! Just shut up!" He stood there as if waiting for a reply that did not come. Stumbling over the corpse, he walked on. Leaning over another body lying broken on the rocks, he reached down and grasped the stiff hand.

"John Skydancer, Tannerman, Inc.," he said, introducing himself in his most professional manner. "I'm sorry I'm late, Mr. Black Two Bears." He shook the stiff hand of the corpse vigorously. "Ran into a little turbulence over the mountains."

That struck Skydancer as being immensely funny. He broke into a fit of hysterical laughter. "Thought we'd have a little dinner and a few drinks before we get your old John Hancock, huh?"

"There's more than just this contract at stake here, Skydancer." Skyler's voice rang very clearly in Skydancer's mind.

Skydancer nodded shrewdly and continued to address the dead man. "No, no . . . don't you worry about a little old thing, Black Two Bears, even though this waiver-of-rights contract is so one-sided I had to title it *Grand Theft, Genocide!* Get it?" Skydancer looked to the corpse for approval.

"Get it? You'll be committing a felony when you sign it!" Sky-dancer fell down beside the corpse, doubled over with laughter.

His hands went out and grabbed a piece of scorched material that was once a business suit and pulled the body next to him. Face to face he said, "It's . . . it's so one-sided, Black Two Bears, it . . . it violates the Geneva Convention." Skydancer was laughing so hard his sides hurt.

The corpse shuddered and the head that lay crumbled on its right shoulder moved. The sightless eyes blinked. The head centered itself on its shattered neck and the lips opened.

"It will soon be over, soon . . . the sickness . . . inside . . . soon."

Skydancer's hands sprang back from the body of the corpse. The body slid back to rest against the rocks. The mouth continued to move.

Skydancer clutched at his throat, strangling, the laughter dying inside him. The face of the corpse was smiling, or so it seemed, nodding at him. Skydancer's face was a mask of terror.

The dead lips whispered. "Soon . . . the mountain . . . You belong to her . . . She's coming for you . . . soon . . ."

"No!" Skydancer shrieked, falling back in horror.

"Yes," whispered the corpse. "Soon . . . soon."

Then the wavering image stabilized into the pale, white, frozen death that was reality. Then back again. And now one of the corpse's mangled arms moved, broken fingers extended, reaching for him.

"You belong . . . with us . . . Come." The hand seemed to brush Skydancer's face, and in that moment, the delirium, if delirium it was, passed.

The corpse was a tumbled heap on the rocks, head askew on its shattered neck, eyes closed, lips sealed. Skydancer's horror was not lessened. His mind reeled. The reality was no less terrifying than the dream.

He scrabbled backwards, crawling in the snow, falling, clawing the rocks in his haste to get away from the corpse. He no longer knew what was real and what was not. Voices seemed to sing in his head.

The mountain seemed to rise up around him on all sides. The trees seemed to tower above him, to stretch upward, impossibly close to the sun. The wind was cold and alive with something as big as the world. The mountain seemed to move at him like a charging animal, like a creature of the nightlands. His vision was blurred, and he struggled to rise, to resist the force that engulfed him.

He stood somehow and threw his head back and the warring tides within him came together and something in him snapped, something that moved in darkness, changed. And the expression on his face changed slowly from fear, from madness and despair to something altogether new, a kind of anger, an anger that had slept in him all of his years.

He raised a clenched fist as if threatening the mountain. "You can't do this to me . . . No more!" His face was a mask of fury. "NOOO!"

He took a step, moving through the wreckage, seeking an enemy he could not see. He kicked debris and scattered bits of metal out of his path. The wind picked up, came singing across the clearing as if trying to match his own fury.

The scrap of dangling steel banged in the wind again. He picked up a rock and hurled it at the incessant racket. "Damn you!" The rock fell short, rolling away.

On he ran, kicking and overturning anything in his path that would move, a different kind of madman now. Stopping, his ragged breathing and thudding heart loud in his ears, he glared at the mountain. "Is this your worst?" His eyes glowed with fire. "You hear me? Is this your worst?"

He laughed loudly and raised his arms over his head. "You've had your shot. Now it's my turn."

As if in answer, the wind rose to a howl, tearing at Skydancer's tattered clothes. Skydancer exulted in the blast of wind, shaking his fists. "Well, I'm waiting!" He picked up another rock and heaved it at the mountain. "Come on! What's next? Another tempting glimpse of an airplane? Another shot at the cougar? Another madman with a gun? Come on, what's next?"

Skydancer kicked a shoe out of his path. There was still a foot in it.

"Why not another Red Hawk? Huh? Come on, you can do better than that! It's only me! How about that black cougar? Why don't you bring back the cougar?"

His voice became a defiant scream. "COME ON, DAMNIT! I'M WAITING!"

He stood there on the skyline, tattered clothes billowing in the fierce mountain wind. Skydancer never felt more alive in his life.

"What? Tired of trying to kill me?" The wind shifted and the piece of metal answered him with a *clang*. He turned his head and looked at it.

"Shut up! I'm talking here!"

The wind ceased at once. The piece of banging metal was stilled.

Skydancer smiled.

And he set his jaw and strode purposefully and confidently up the gorge, looking neither to the left nor to the right. A pair of eyes watched him move away from the wreckage. They burned with secret knowledge.

Skydancer moved as if his legs were wings. And he walked now with a new and terrible strength.

33

Fiske reined his horse in at the mouth of a narrow canyon. Group C spread out around him along the sides of the cut. One of the riders to his right leaned out from his mount and picked something out of the brush. Fiske watched him turn in the saddle and wave. The deputy signaled with his hand and trotted to the excited man.

"Found something, Sheriff," the rider said as he dismounted and walked to Fiske. Leaning down, Fiske took the objects out of the man's hand and held them up. He scrutinized the ragged cloth and said, "Looks like a pair of socks."

"Yeah, and that's bloodstains on 'em."

"What the hell is a pair of bloody socks doin' in the brush?" inquired Fiske, more to himself than to the equally bewildered rider.

"Could have been a camper or a hiker with blisters. Just threw 'em away. No telling how long they been here."

"Yeah," mused Fiske. "You're probably right." He kicked his horse and moved out as the other man remounted. At the bottom of the canyon he turned and stuffed the socks into his saddlebags. As he swiveled back around, something caught his eye. He stopped, pulling back hard on the reins. He stared ahead.

In the branches of a tree directly in front of him was a pair of Jockey shorts.

Red Hawk stared at the determined figure that marched up the gorge. Below his sightless eyes the bottom half of his face was a pulpy red gash. His head was at a slight angle, neck broken, ripped throat a mass of twisted cartilage above his gouged chest.

Skydancer came up along the fuselage dragging Red Hawk's backpack over the ground. He stopped when he saw the body, recognizing Red Hawk's back and what was left of his shirt. He shook his head and laughed as he spotted the pile of loot on the rock. "Looks like you really cashed in this time."

He let the pack fall and walked to the rock. He tossed his own much too thin topcoat away and grabbed the corners of Red Hawk's sheepskin jacket and yanked, sending the pile of looted valuables flying over the ground in all directions.

He put on the coat and stood there for a second, enjoying the feel of the sheepskin lining, knowing it would be warm. He remembered sleeping on a sheepskin rug when he was little.

"Not a bad fit," he said to the corpse of Red Hawk. "I thank you for the use of it." Then he looked down at his feet and then looked at Red Hawk's boots.

"I'm sorry, I think I need your boots too." He knelt and removed the dead man's boots. It was not exactly a happy task. Surprisingly, the boots were a perfect fit. He threw his dress shoes away and pulled his pants down over the tops of the boots. He saw the knife off to one side and he picked it up too.

He took Red Hawk's belt, fastened it around his waist and then slipped the knife into the sheath.

"Okay, Red Hawk, let's see if we can find the gun. No, don't get up, friend. I think I can manage on my own now." He walked around until he spotted the gun in the snow. He picked up the .45 and wiped it on his coat. Then he brought it up and sighted down the blue steel barrel at the fuselage.

He pulled the trigger. Nothing happened.

"Ah yes, I remember some things about guns too." He examined the gun, found what he was looking for and thumbed off the safety near the trigger guard. Smiling, he aimed again and fired.

Fiske was coming up a ravine about a hundred yards ahead of the main group when he heard the faint sound of a shot. He pulled back hard on the reins and tried to listen over the puffing of his horse. The man who had discovered the socks was beside him. Fiske looked over and said, "You hear that?"

"Heard something, but it was kinda muffled."

Fiske listened for a moment, then said, "Gunshot."

The other man shook his head. "Heavy snow breaking a tree limb, or a rockslide. You hear it all the time."

Fiske pointed off to the right. "It came from that way." He turned his horse. The other man did not move.

"That'd take us off the heading we're supposed to follow, Sheriff."

Fiske stopped and looked at the ranger. "Get 'em in line and follow me. Pass the word to be as quiet as possible."

The ranger nodded and rode off. Fiske removed his revolver from its holster and held it above his head. He fired and the sound of the shot was muted by the ravine. He fired twice more but the wind was against him and the reports died in the air.

Pocketing the gun, Skydancer picked up Red Hawk's black hat, which had fallen in the rocks. Setting it on his head, he modeled it for the dead man. "How's that?" He pulled the front of the hat lower over his eyes, cowboy fashion. "Better?"

He straightened and pushed the hat back on his head. Then he took the hat off. "No. I don't think I want to look like a cowboy. Maybe that's been the trouble with my life. Maybe I've been the cowboy from Harvard when I should have been the Indian from somewhere else instead."

He looked down at Red Hawk. "You don't look so good. You look like you might have got caught with some kind of white man's disease. You think so?"

He stood over the body of Red Hawk. "What's wrong? Cat got your tongue?"

He turned away. "Even my bad jokes aren't funny." He pulled the backpack upright and braced it against the fuselage next to Red Hawk's body. Untying the top flap, he began to rummage through it. He came up with a spare shirt, a blanket, socks and some dried beef. Digging deeper, he pulled out a handful of candy bars. Unwrapping one, he took a grateful bite. Chewing slowly, he savored the sharp tang of chocolate. He looked down at Red Hawk, remembering how the dead man had treated him.

He offered the candy bar to him. "Want a bite?" Red Hawk's eyes stared uncomprehendingly up at the sky.

"It's white man's food. Very life-sustaining," said Skydancer, and he laughed.

He dropped the candy wrapper on the ground and wiped his mouth with the back of his hand. Going back to the pack, he took out a box of shells for the long-lost rifle and two spare clips for the pistol. Tossing the box of shells into a snowbank, he put the clips in his pocket with the gun.

The next item to appear was a hand compass. It was broken. He held it up for Red Hawk to see. "I guess it never points north when it's broken, huh? Oh well, never mind." He raised a hand to his brow and squinted into the sun. "Assuming the sun still sets in the west, and what I remember from being a kid, that moss always grows thickest on the north side of trees, then . . . ." He turned to look past the far end of the plane wreck. "Then that's the way to go to get out of here. I guess I won't need the compass after all." He rose and stuffed the equipment back into the pack. Sticking a piece of beef in his mouth, he swung the pack up over his shoulders. He stared off into the distance. He had suddenly realized that there were a lot of things about his childhood that he remembered, more than he realized he knew. That part of him that was Indian wasn't as buried as he had thought it was.

"So long," he said, waving at the dead body of Red Hawk. "I think it's time I found someplace else to be."

He walked away, heading southeast. There was something about this mountain that seemed to touch a part of him he thought long dead. In a crazy sort of way he felt like he had fallen into one of the old stories the people of his tribe used to tell. It seemed like the world they talked about had suddenly made itself real and he moved in it, that somehow it was something that he had to fight, to overcome.

As he walked out of the far end of the gorge, Fiske entered at its mouth and dismounted. He looked at the beginning of the wreckage and the skin around his eyes tightened. He motioned to the radioman. "Take your rig up to the high ground and tell 'em we found it. Tell 'em it don't look good."

It took the radioman the better part of an hour to find a spot of ridge high enough to receive. The operator on duty took another fifteen minutes to locate Tucker, who was eating at a diner in town. The colonel immediately ordered the big copters into the air and in forty-five minutes they were touching down in a clearing a quarter of a mile from the crash site.

In those two hours the sun had almost set. And John Skydancer had penetrated deep into the thick underbrush of the mountains, now five long miles from the wreck . . . and safety.

34

The clear running water pooled a yard deep on the bank side of the jumbled logs that blocked the stream. The last rays of waning sunlight reflected off its ebbs and currents. Skydancer had built a fire in a depression on the bank. The covelike dell was walled with brush, shielding the glowing embers from the wind.

The backpack rested against a log near the fire, wide open, Red Hawk's belongings thrown haphazardly around it. Skydancer had spread the blanket in the branches of a tree above the fire. The woolen square warmed over the flames.

He was naked to the waist. Removing the last of his clothing, the ragged and tattered suit trousers, he walked forward into the water up to his ankles. He grimaced as the icy stream swirled about his sore feet. Holding his breath, he waded out until the water lapped at his kneecaps. Shivering violently, he took another step, then fell rather than dived into the pool.

Surfacing, he sputtered, his body shocked from the chill. He ducked his head again, then bobbed, shaking himself like a wet dog. Standing the freeze for as long as he could, he began to wash away the blood and grime. One last submersion and he stumbled for the bank, toward the beckoning fire.

Grabbing the heated blanket, he pulled it around his quivering frame. He pat-dried himself, rubbing briskly over his strained muscles. Dry, he swung out the blanket around the fire and stood there, drinking in the heat. Sitting down, he tucked it around him and began finger-combing his hair. He ran his long fingernails through the bushy swatch of gray-black and pulled out burrs and twigs.

His beard, always thin, was next. He picked something small

and alive out of it and squashed it between his fingertips. Satisfied with his grooming, he dropped the blanket, rose and walked to the pile of clothing.

He mentally thanked Red Hawk for including a change of clothing as he rummaged through the pile. He pulled a pair of too large boxer shorts up over his bruised knees and hunted for an undershirt. Finding none, he put on a dark McGregor shirt, its rough material scratchy on his arms and chest.

The Levi's were too big at the waist by several sizes but he fastened the wide belt and cinched it tight. The pullover sweater went on next, followed by two pairs of stockings to keep out the cold.

As he dressed, he was perfectly calm. He had made up his mind what was to become of him. He went about the task of survival with a mechanical precision. He was a changed man.

He tucked the .45 into his belt and donned the coat. Checking the pockets, he made sure the spare ammo was secure. Then he put the black hat on over his damp hair. For the first time in longer than he could remember he felt a small degree of comfort. After such an ordeal, most would have succumbed to languor and lost themselves in exhausted sleep in the sultry glow of the fire.

Not Skydancer. That portion of his mind that screamed for rest was violently subjugated by an expanding feeling of ego that now dominated his being. A psychiatrist might have told him that a long-pent-up dual personality had emerged, a built-in defense mechanism conjured up to protect the whole. Over a hot cup of coffee in a nice warm office the doctor might have told him many things to aid him in taking a firmer grip on the reality of the situation.

Skydancer, being what he was now, would have punched him in the mouth.

He took another candy bar from the pack. Dropping the paper into the fire, he swallowed the candy in two gulps. He put the rest of the gear back into the pack and hefted it to his shoulders. After kicking snow on the fire he stopped at the stream for a drink. Then he walked into the woods.

On the line of a ridge the trees were sparse and he made good time. He moved purposefully, avoiding rough ground and staying to the open spaces on the ridge. The drop-off below him grew thick and dark. A hundred yards to his left, on the other side of the gorge and paralleling his course, was the cat.

It melded with the blackness, keeping abreast of the walking man. It looked for an opening in the thicket wall from which to attack its unsuspecting quarry. There was none. It tossed its head and growled.

The moon was out as Skydancer approached the base of a high cliff. He stopped and surveyed the graded slope that angled sharply upward to a sheer granite wall. At the base of the wall, about fifteen feet above him, was a dark spot he recognized as a shallow cave. It was high enough to keep him out of reach of whatever prowled the night yet not too high for him to climb to, and it was defensible, after a fashion.

He started up the grade, hand over hand, grasping at the bushes and rocks as he ascended. The cat watched from a distance, cut off by a wide ravine that ended at the thicket wall. Skydancer's back was to the monster but had he been looking in that direction, the darkness of the ravine would have revealed nothing to his untrained eyes.

The cat backed up a dozen feet, glared at the climbing man, then launched itself at the ravine. The abyss was at least twenty feet wide, with the thicket wall beginning again on the opposite side and continuing another ten. The height of the brush there was at least that of a man.

The cat soared across the ravine, cleared the brush barricade neatly and landed silently on the other side. The ground between it and Skydancer was clear.

Skydancer reached the cave mouth and turned to look back. The cat froze, another patch of black in the night.

Skydancer pulled brush from the hillside next to the cave. In a few minutes he had a sizable pile of twigs and branches. He removed a box of matches from his coat and kindled a fire.

The light from the fire did not show for a great distance but the cat lowered its huge body to the ground and placed its head on its forepaws. There it stayed, watching.

Skydancer fed the fire. The light reflected the dullness in his eyes. His hands moved unconsciously as he dropped the pieces of wood into the flames.

He built the fire high, then settled back against the pack. Pulling the blanket around his shoulders, he closed his eyes. The pistol was in his hands.

The sun rose over the mountains, glinting off the bright aluminum of a fixed-wing aircraft. The plane circled above a growing camp at the foot of the gorge that held the wreckage. Below, in the clearing, a helicopter landed to join the two already on the ground. The camp was alive with activity. Searchers poked around the debris, sifting the snow and bits of metal for bodies.

A long row of plastic-bagged mounds rested in the clearing next to the copters. Stretcher bearers made numerous trips between the mounds and the gorge.

Lloyd Fiske walked through the now crowded gorge and surveyed the remains of the 727. He stopped by a low rock and sat, tipping his hat back on his head. Two airmen moved past him to the fuselage and set a stretcher and a plastic bag down on the ground next to Red Hawk's body. The sightless eyes of the corpse stared at Fiske.

The deputy looked at the ruined body and his mouth felt dry. He licked his lips and looked away as another man came up and plopped down on the rock beside him. "A bit gruesome, huh, Sheriff?" said Norton Harper, an FAA inspector who had been one of the first on the scene the night before.

Fiske nodded. "I thought I'd seen just about everything, but this makes a man want to . . ." He trailed off as he looked around at the broken bodies.

"No, it's not pretty, but you get used to it after the first few times." Harper leaned down and scratched at the base of the rock. A small bit of green showed through the snow. He plucked at it and came up with a hundred-dollar bill. "Well."

Fiske furrowed his brow when he saw the money. Harper folded the bill neatly in half and dropped it into a small bag he carried. As he did, he noticed the deputy's look.

"Hell," he said. "That's not unusual. Impact like this does some crazy things. I remember once I found a set of dentures embedded—"

Fiske stopped him with a wave of his hand and rose, a sickly expression on his face. Harper watched him walk to a boulder and lean over it. The FAA man shook his head and walked away in the opposite direction.

While Fiske was coloring the snow the two men with the stretcher lifted what was left of Red Hawk's body and slid it into the long black bag.

35

In Northpass, Skyler stepped from the command trailer and walked down the road to the motor court. He reached the flaking door and paused, rehearsing his words in his mind.

Then he knocked and was told to enter.

Pamela sat on the bed, the phone braced against her ear. She toyed with an earring she had removed as she talked. "And three bottles of scotch, Peter Dawson if you have it. Ice, at least two bags. Do you take Visa or MasterCharge? Of course, I want it now, idiot!" She slammed the phone down.

Skyler stood at the foot of the bed, not saying anything.

She stared up at him expectantly.

"Well?" Her voice was calm.

"They found it," said Skyler.

"It meaning the plane, Skydancer's body or your goddamn papers?"

"I mean the plane."

"And?"

"It's bad. They can't be positive until they bring all the bodies in, but . . ."

"But what?"

Skyler looked out the window, avoiding her eyes. "The preliminary body count tallies with the passenger list."

"That's it, then," she said, a note of relief in her voice. "I need a drink! God, do I need a drink! You didn't see Michael out there anywhere, did you? I sent the moron out to get some booze, at least an hour ago. What's taking him so damn long? The stupid bastard probably got lost falling off a barstool somewhere."

"I posted a reward for the documents but it doesn't look good. I offered fifty thousand dollars' reward. Caused quite a scramble. The sheriff's office sent me an official complaint, said they couldn't afford to spare any men from the task of moving the bodies out, but the reward money cost them almost all of their non-military personnel. It's not my fault if people would rather make money than move bodies, is it?"

"Money talks, and when money talks, people listen, right, Father?"

"Something like that," said Skyler. "Well, it's resolved any way you look at it. The plane is down, Skydancer is dead and the papers may or may not be recovered. We've done as much as we can do. We can pack up and head for home now."

"And miss out on a widow's most sacred duty, identifying the remains of my dearly beloved? Fat chance. I owe the poor bastard something, don't I?"

"You don't have to run it into the ground. He's dead, and you know as well as I do, you can't do anything more for him now."

Skyler took her by the shoulders, holding her tightly. She trembled in his grasp. "You really did love him, didn't you? This is all just one big tough act, isn't it? You're acting hard as hell on the outside but you're dying inside."

"Maybe," she said, unable to meet his eyes. "I don't know how to cry, Daddy." It was one of the few times she had ever called him by that name. "You taught me lots of things. Mostly you taught me how to win at something or someone, but you never taught me how to lose at something or someone. I feel so damn empty inside."

"Maybe you'd feel better if you drank less and got rid of that overgrown ape, Michael." It was the wrong thing to say and he knew it regretfully the moment he spoke it.

"Oh, shut up, Skyler! How would you know anything about how I'd feel? I'll run my life and you run yours."

She was back to being hard again and he knew he had made her that way.

"Well, then I'm sorry, Pamela. I guess I'll be heading back to Denver, catch the first plane out. You take care of yourself, daughter."

He was at the door then, a lonely man who couldn't find the words he had meant to say. I've failed her, he thought.

"Listen to me, Pamela. They can't identify most of the bodies.

The plane exploded. There was a fireball. It's not something . . . Well, it won't be pleasant. Do yourself a favor. Better yet, do *me* a favor. Come home with me."

The door opened behind his back and Michael came in with a sack full of whiskey bottles.

She acted like he hadn't even spoken.

"Jesus! Whiskey! I'm dying for a drink!" said Pamela.

"Hi, Mr. Tannerman. How are you? Any news yet?" Michael said, holding out a hand to shake hands.

"Have a good flight, Skyler," said Pamela.

Skyler looked at her one final time, then pushed past Michael, going abruptly through the door, ignoring Michael's outstretched hand.

"Is your father mad at me or something?" asked Michael, looking puzzled.

Pamela laughed unhappily as she took a bottle from him, uncapped it and belted down a healthy slug. "I think it's or something," she said. "Let's get drunk."

36

The sun was high as the late John Skydancer made his way along a narrow ledge overlooking a drop-off of a hundred feet. His face was pressed against the rock. Both hands were outstretched, palms flat on the smooth granite. He felt his way slowly, unable to look directly down because of the position of his head.

"Easy now . . . easy." He talked to himself as he maneuvered the narrow shelf, his voice calm, rational. "Only a few more feet to go . . . Don't blow it now."

As he pushed his left foot forward, the toe of his boot caught on a snag of stone. He slipped, losing his balance for a moment, the bulky backpack weighing him down, trying to pull him into the fissure below.

He sucked in his breath and scrambled for a toehold. His boot scraped the cliff, causing loose stones to fall away. Reaching for a piece of brush, he lunged and managed to grab it, securing himself on the slim reed that grew out of the rock itself.

Settling himself back on the ledge, he proceeded to inch his way on. "Nobody said it was gonna be easy . . . Just a few . . . more . . ." He reached for another handhold, a cleft in the rock face. Holding on to the almost invisible crack, he attempted to swing his left leg to an open space on the ledge that was as wide as his body.

Swinging his body onto the relative safety of the wide spot, he sighed. "There, wasn't all that hard. Just takes a little practice." His breathing was deep but controlled as he looked up to get his bearings. The rock face above him angled away from him as it climbed upward. He gauged the distance to the bushes and small trees that grew above his outstretched fingers. They were yards away. He had no choice but to go on across the face of the cliff.

He again pressed his cheek to the cool stone and began to move sideways. "One step at a time . . . easy . . . almost there."

As he uttered the last word, his foot slipped. Loose rock tumbled under his boot and he went down painfully on one knee. He still clutched the side of the cliff. "Damn!"

Pulling his foot back carefully, he lost hold with his left hand. Now only his right hand and right leg kept him from falling.

He looked down, fear in his eyes.

Thirty feet above him, concealed by brush, sat the black cougar. The big cat watched the teetering figure as it began to slide forward on its belly, coming out to meet Skydancer.

Skydancer fought desperately to regain a handhold. He swayed from side to side. He tried to regain a foothold with his left foot. A laugh rose over his hard breathing.

"Here's another fine mess you've gotten us . . ."

His other foot slipped. Skydancer screamed as he plummeted over the edge.

37

The cat watched Skydancer disappear from sight over the edge of the cliff. It came to its feet and padded its way purposefully through the bushes, leaping the last ten feet easily and coming to rest where Skydancer had stood minutes before.

Below, four feet down the sheer cliff face, Skydancer dangled in the breeze. One aluminum strut of the backpack was hooked on a bush that extended at a forty-five-degree angle upward from the side of the smooth wall. The nylon strap on the strut was looped around the fragile protrusion and, as Skydancer thrashed, the bush bowed to the law of gravity. It slumped downward under his weight, then slipped.

Skydancer jerked in the air. His hands clawed for purchase on the slippery stone. His eyes fixed on the snagged loop and he stopped all movement.

He hung about eighteen inches out from the face of the cliff. Slowly and cautiously, he began to reach upward with one hand.

He couldn't use both hands because of the angle of the backpack. He moved very slowly. The pack maintained its precarious hold but his arm was encumbered by the chest straps. He couldn't reach the bush. His fingers slashed the air inches from the bush and he began to swing. He looked down at the crevice below and ceased all movement, bringing his hand back to his chest. He was perspiring freely and his hands were getting damp.

As he raised his head, looking for another solution, the pack slipped again. The loop came off the top branch of the bush and rehooked on a lower limb. Skydancer jerked like a puppet, falling a foot before the nylon caught and held. He hazarded another upward glance. The strain on the weakened tree was pulling it out by the roots.

Only a scant few inches remained before the loop was free and he became nothing but a stain on the rocks below. He wiped a sweaty hand on his coat. Then he reached carefully across his chest with his left hand and began to loosen the right shoulder strap of the pack. The loop quivered with the movement and slipped again.

He continued to work one-handed until he had the strap free. With the weight removed from the right side of his body he tilted downward, held only by one remaining strap. His arm now free, he extended it upward and felt along the smooth surface of the cliff for a handhold. He found none.

The effort caused him to begin swinging wildly now and the motion of his body shook the bush. The pack eased down, lowering him a few more inches closer to the rugged ground below. He attempted to reach the branch above him with his fingers. He almost touched it. Using the motion of his body to swing upward, he tried again. "Come on . . ." He missed.

He strained with all his might and braced a knee against the cliff, finally touching the branch with one finger. "Ahh." He began to gain a hold on the branch. There. He had it. He pulled himself upward and looked right into the glaring eyes of the cat.

He froze, his face painted with shock. The cat screamed, this time like a tortured woman, a piercing sound that echoed in the canyon.

Skydancer's hands began to shake.

Steeling himself, he fumbled with the center button of his coat, not taking his eyes off the cat.

He felt the fetid breath of the carnivore on his face and fought the urge to be sick. He was having difficulty with the coat button. The bush shook with the movement.

Suddenly he began to laugh insanely. Looking up at the hissing thing above him, he said. "We're going to have to stop meeting like this." In answer, the cat roared and dropped forward. The cougar viciously swiped at Skydancer's head with razor-sharp claws.

The raking talons missed his face by scant inches.

"Nice try," said Skydancer. He had the coat loose now and he pulled the pistol from his belt. The cat made another pass. It missed, but just barely. Skydancer thumbed back the hammer of the gun and brought it up. "Now it's my turn," he said evenly.

The cat turned and was gone, moving so fast that Skydancer didn't see it.

He squeezed the trigger. The recoil of the blast pushed him out from the cliff and he slammed back hard. The loop came free. He made a desperate grab for the bush with his free hand and managed to hold on as the weight of the pack pulled him out over the gorge. Panting, he slid the pistol back in his belt and reached up with his other hand to grab the bush. He had a firm hold on it but he was hampered by the bobbing pack.

He loosened one hand, quickly unsnapping the remaining strap. The pack slid off and plummeted downward, twisting end over end into the canyon below. He watched it hit the side of a ridge and break open, splattering its contents everywhere. He laughed. "You haven't got me yet." With both hands on the bush and his feet braced on the cliff he laboriously pulled himself upward. He stopped a few inches below the ledge and scraped a foothold in the shale. Balancing himself, he took the pistol and slowly raised his head, the gun alongside his cheek.

He pushed the gun forward and looked onto the ledge.

The cat was gone.

Skydancer walked through a glade surrounded by low hills. In the valley, grass pushed its way through the shrinking snow. He left footprints in a winding trail as he moved confidently ahead.

Stopping, he reached into his coat pocket and withdrew the compass. Looking at it, then into the sky, he changed direction slightly, heading for a rise a few hundred yards away. His stride was unhurried but he glanced over his shoulder every so often, his look not frightened but cautious.

A small stream cascaded over stones in the center of the glade. A rabbit sat beside it, dipping its paws in the moving water. It licked at its damp fur, then dipped again.

The rabbit was plump and white against the background of green grass that grew along the bank of the stream. The line of grass extended to snow-topped boulders at the beginning of the cut. On one of the boulders Skydancer leaned forward and sighted the pistol.

He fired and the slug kicked up a plume of water in front of the startled rabbit. It jumped back and disappeared into the rocks. A small wisp of smoke rose from the barrel of the gun as Skydancer lowered it and made his way to the stream. He looked down at the spot where the rabbit had been. "Skydancer, the great off-white hunter! Ah the hell with it, probably wouldn't have liked the taste of rabbit anyway."

Standing at the edge of the running water, he looked hungrily at the paw prints in the mud. "Well, at least let me buy you a drink," he said as he knelt and scooped a handful of water to his mouth.

By late afternoon he had found a bush bristling with spring berries. He picked the swollen gems and stuffed them into his mouth, gulping madly. With the edge off his hunger he chewed more slowly, enjoying the tartness of the berries, rolling them around in his mouth. Then he turned up his collar against the cold and moved on, his pockets bulging with berries.

Crossing a meadow, he approached a stand of trees. The sun was beginning to disappear behind them, so he decided to make camp. He selected a bare spot of ground well into the trees and circled it, collecting firewood. After several minutes he had gathered a decent supply of almost dry scraps and he dug a shallow depression in the soil beneath one of the trees.

The loss of the backpack had cost him most of his supplies and as the fire glowed in the approaching darkness he took stock of his possessions. From the pocket of the coat he withdrew the hand compass, spare magazines for the .45 and two mangled candy bars.

He leaned back against the tree and ate one of the bars, his eyes watching the flames lick at the twigs in the fire. From the other pocket he took a handful of berries and munched on his dessert. He must have dozed for some time, because when he came awake the fire was dwindling. Rising, he stretched his stiff frame and walked into the woods to look for more kindling.

He picked up bark and scraps of branches as he walked until his arms were full. Balancing the pile of firewood under his chin, he ducked a low branch and came back into the clearing.

Face to face with the black cougar.

A snarling black demon of sudden implacable death. With one smooth motion he threw the firewood and went for his gun. The pile of branches struck the cat, taking it by surprise. It jumped sideways to avoid the clattering branches. That was all Skydancer needed.

Falling backward, he cocked the gun as he hit the ground, rolled over and slid behind the bole of a tree. As he rolled out on the other side, he was firing. When his eyes recovered from the flaming muzzle blasts he scanned the clearing through the sights of the gun.

No cougar.

He went to his elbows, gun extended in both hands, perfectly still. His eyes searched the dark trees that danced in the light from the dying fire. The only sound was that of his labored breathing.

Suddenly, the growl of the cat came from behind him. For a moment a knife of fear twisted in his stomach. Then his eyes cleared and a thin smile edged its way across his face. He did not move, keeping the gun pointed away from the noise to his rear. He sighted carefully down the barrel at the clump of brush directly in front of him. And waited.

The sound behind him died. There was a slight movement in the brush in front of him. The smile broke into a wide grin. The long body of the cat came out of the brush into the sights of the .45. Skydancer fired.

The slug snapped a branch a foot above the cat's head and it hissed angrily.

Turning, it crashed away into the tree, running from the hunted man.

Skydancer stood and laughed deeply and waved the smoking gun in the direction of the fleeing cat. "Come on back and try again, damnit!" He fought for breath between his shouts.

"The plane crash couldn't kill me! Red Hawk couldn't kill me!"

He crossed the clearing, raising his arms in triumph.

"And you won't get me either. I'm goddamn invincible!"

He turned in a circle, firing into the trees, pulling the trigger over and over again. The shots shook the clearing until only a hollow clicking could be heard. He stood there, eyes flashing, squeezing the trigger of an empty gun.

Under the floodlights at the crash site, plastic-bagged corpses were being loaded into the waiting helicopters. Fiske stood on the lip of the gorge watching the activity in the clearing. The moon was high and the entire scene of the wreckage could be seen from his vantage point. He stood alone, wondering what the hell he had gotten himself involved in.

As he contemplated the carnage below, one of the copters fired up. Its exhaust popped and its silver blades began whirring in the moonlight. Fiske listened to the engine gain speed and turned his head to the mountains. For a second he thought he heard popping sounds coming from the southeast, a series of firecracker-like snaps. The roar of the copter rose in intensity as the awkward aircraft lifted off. The downdraft from its spinning blades caused the trees to lean away from the clearing.

The loud whirling sound drowned out whatever it was Fiske thought he heard.

38

The sun rose over the field beside the Northpass General Store. The large fenced area had been converted into a temporary clearing-house for the dead. Bodies were being downloaded from idling helicopters and stacked in long rows on the far side of the store. Three medical examiners from the county coroner's office, assisted by a number of civilian volunteers, marked the plastic bags with large red tags. Each tag had a black number on it.

The officials scribbled grease-penciled notes on the tags: approximate body weight and height, sex if discernible and any scars or marks that would aid later in a more positive identification. After the initial inspection the corpses were shuttled by ambulances and military vehicles to a large feed-storage barn at the other end of the field. There photographs and fingerprints were taken and personal belongings sorted in an effort to put a name to each body.

The chief medical examiner, Martin Lusky, a harried man in his sixties, stood talking to his people outside the barn as Pamela and Michael drove up in their rented car. Michael got out, opened the door for Pamela and the two approached the group. They waited for a break in the conversation as Lusky ranted at his aides.

"I don't give a rat's ass what the transportation problems are!" the doctor was yelling at a younger man with a clipboard. "I want these bodies processed before dark. You see to it that you get the vehicles you need if you have to steal them!"

The man with the clipboard nodded and moved off toward the entrance to the barn. Lusky shouted after him, "Talk to Tucker! He'll get you more trucks if he has to airlift them in. Tell him Lusky needs a favor." He turned to Pamela, then as an afterthought said, "Knowing Tucker, he'll probably send the boy back in uniform."

Pamela smiled weakly. "Excuse me, Mr. Lusky. I'm Pamela Skydancer. My husband was aboard the plane."

Lusky frowned and looked past her to the well-dressed man who stood slightly behind her. "I'm sorry to hear that, Mrs. Skydancer." Turning back, he continued. "I'm very busy, Mrs. Skydancer. If you'll check with my office in a couple of days we should be able to give you more information."

Lusky pivoted and began to walk away. Pamela grabbed his arm and swung him around. "Now just a minute, Doctor. We've been here for a long time. The least you can do is talk to me!"

Lusky shook her hand off and looked back at Michael. Making a decision, he said, "I'm sorry, lady. It's just that in a situation like this there's not a hell of a lot I can offer in the way of condolences. I just do my job and try not to get involved with relatives. It makes my life a great deal easier."

"I understand, Doctor," Pamela said softly. "Could you just tell me when we'll be able to take possession of my husband's body?"

Lusky felt the urge to yell at the woman but controlled it. "I really don't have too many positive IDs right now." He turned and shouted at another man who was walking through the rows of bodies with a stack of red tags in his hand. "Ribeck? You got a Skydancer on your confirmed list?"

Ribeck flipped through several pages of notes. "Got a Skykowalski, Anita. That's the closest," he replied.

"I'm afraid that's the best I can offer you right now," Lusky said to Pamela. "I'm sorry."

"I can understand your problems, sir. I have several of my own. How soon do you think it will be before you can help me?"

Lusky lost control. "Look, lady!" he shouted. "I got over seventy-five stiffs in there charred so bad their own mothers wouldn't know them! I got one bag that's just limbs! You want to sift through them and see if you come up with anything you recognize?"

Michael stepped between them. "That's enough, buddy."

Lusky sighed. "Yeah, yeah, yeah . . . but you get the idea now? There's nothing I can do for you, at least not for a few days."

Pamela stared daggers at Lusky as Michael put his arm comfortingly on her shoulder. Lusky shook his head and walked back to the open double doors of the barn. Stopping, he said, "The body count agrees with that of the passenger and crew lists, in case you had any crazy hopes."

Michael led Pamela back to the car. "Well, I can't say I like the son of a bitch," he said. "But I guess he leveled with us. Let's get our stuff and head back to Denver. Guess it would be best, don't you think?"

"No."

"What?"

"Maybe by tomorrow morning they'll be able to tell us more. Besides, you want us to get married, don't you, Michael? Well, we've got to have a death certificate first, don't we?"

Michael nodded. "Oh yeah. I never thought of that."

Pamela looked disgusted. "Of course, Skydancer may walk out of those woods over there and say, 'I'm going to blow your brains out, you faithless . . .' " She bit her lip. "Damnit, let's get the hell out of here!"

Michael stopped and put his arms on her shoulders. He looked into her eyes. "Look, Pamela, the guy loved you. And once, I guess you loved him too, but he couldn't help what happened to him any more than we could help ourselves, so what say? This is my idea. We can leave tomorrow and they can just send us the death certificate already. What say?"

Pamela leaned over and kissed him. "What's wrong, Michael? Can't you think of anything interesting to do in our hotel room anymore?"

His face lit up and he moved against her.

From the corner of the barn, Lusky watched the two embrace and spat with pure disgust on the ground.

39

On the mountain, Skydancer walked through the trees, nibbling on a handful of berries. He looked up at the bright sun as he chewed mechanically. The berries were harsh and bitter but they were nourishment all the same.

Skydancer's face was becoming deeply tanned by the sun shining through the thin mountain air. The lines around his eyes were deeper, darker.

There was a change not only in his face but in the way he moved, the way he carried himself. He no longer walked like a man carrying a briefcase in a crowded department store.

His chin was stained by berry juice.

He carried his coat slung over one shoulder, hooked with a finger, as he munched the berries out of the palm of his other hand. Sheathed on his left side was Red Hawk's hunting knife. The pistol was tucked in his belt across his stomach. He whistled between swallows.

The black cougar watched Skydancer's approach from behind a patch of scrub brush. His cover was atop a pile of large rocks in front of Skydancer and slightly to the right.

Crouched low in the leaves, the black cougar's shape was indistinguishable from the dark boulders around it.

As Skydancer reached the top of the scarp, he finished the last of the berries. He wiped his hand on his pants. He stopped and looked around in a complete circle. Although he saw nothing, he sensed an out-of-place presence. He turned back to the trail and his eyes centered on the exact spot where the cat waited.

It was impossible for him to see the cat from that distance but he stared at the boulders for a long time. The cat hissed softly and glared at the watcher but it did not move from its hiding place. Skydancer resumed walking toward the boulders. When he was within fifty feet of the hidden cat, without breaking stride he hefted the pistol from his belt, cocking the hammer back with one thumb. He kept the gun more or less out of sight along his side.

The side that faced away from the cat.

The cat observed Skydancer's movement with the .45 and growled, a low sound that Skydancer could not hear, more a low exhaling of hot breath. It seemed to study Skydancer's face as he came closer. Then, as if moved by some force, it slid backwards on its belly and out of Skydancer's path. It growled once and then disappeared into the trees.

An hour later found Skydancer sliding down the side of a rocky gully. As he reached the lower elevations the snow had begun to disappear and the ground was wet with running water. At the bottom of the gully a swollen creek fed by the channels of melting snow surged through fallen trees and polished stone. The water was moving fast and the stream was at least forty feet across.

Skydancer stopped on the near bank and consulted his compass. He raised his eyes to take in the thick foliage that covered the wall of the gully across the rushing stream. Sighing, he looked upstream. Deciding that it was impassable, he turned downstream, looking for a place to cross.

He went a hundred feet and stopped, hampered by the growth on the bank of the creek that was now becoming a small river. Giving up, he retraced his steps and fought his way back up the gully. It narrowed as he progressed upstream, its sides becoming steeper and the brush thicker. Soon he found himself imprisoned by its towering sides.

Around a bend in the stream he spotted a fallen tree whose roots had upended in the muddy bank on his side of the river. The dead tree bridged out over the white froth that cascaded around the sharp rocks in the center of the stream. On the other bank the upper portion of the tree met the top of a slight rise. The ground was clear of obstacles at that point.

Skydancer smiled and walked up on the thick bole of the tree, testing its security by lightly jumping up and down on the end. The tree, over a foot in diameter, shook unreassuringly under his weight. Still he had no choice. He sat on the log and began to slide forward, inching his way, hand over hand, lifting his hips forward and dragging himself ahead again with his hands.

About a fourth of the way across, his hand slipped on the spray-washed wood and he almost went toppling over the side. He caught hold of a stub of a broken branch at the last second. Using that to steady himself, he pulled himself back to the top of the curved tree trunk. He lay flat now, forced to crawl forward now, unable to retreat.

The spray hit him in the face and his hands got damper.

Summoning his courage, he inched painfully forward. The tree trunk became narrower and he lost his balance again. As he fell, he locked his arms and legs around the tree, and ended up dangling like a crude human necklace just inches above the roaring water.

It was a dangerous position to find himself in and he knew it. He grunted and began to squirm ahead, his face splashing in and out of the water. Through spray-glazed eyes he could see the opposite bank nearing and he worked harder, gasping for breath and holding on with all the strength he had left.

He was halfway across when he saw the black cougar, the lurking black death. It moved calmly out of the brush on the bank he was attempting to reach. It stood at the top of the tree buried in the loose dirt of the far bank.

Skydancer took one hand off the log and tried to reach for the gun in his belt. The motion caused him to sway precariously. He grabbed the log with both hands and steadied himself. The sound of his harsh breathing was loud over the swirling water.

The cougar ignored the man hanging in the middle of the log and began to dig at the soil bracing the treetop on the far bank. The top of the tree was only a few inches in diameter where it had lodged in the bank when it fell.

The black cougar worried the dirt, slowly at first, then faster and faster as the loosened dirt caused the tree to shake.

Skydancer could do nothing but stare at the dark one from his upside-down perch. Just watch and try desperately to hold on. The log jerked, slipping closer to the water.

With all his might, he heaved upward, struggling to get atop the log as it settled lower. He made it, gasping with the effort, lying flat on top, facing the black one.

The cougar clawed furiously and piles of dirt slid down the bank into the stream.

It dug furiously and Skydancer could see that it was only a matter of seconds before he would be swimming for it.

He began to slide backwards along the log, humping his body like an earthworm. His progress was grotesquely slow.

The log slipped again and he stopped. He raised his head and shouted over the torrent below, "You are one persistent son of a bitch, I gotta give you that!"

At the sound of Skydancer's yell, the cougar looked up from its labors and growled savagely. Its ears flattened against its massive head and its eyes blazed brilliantly.

Skydancer found the menace, the almost bold challenge in the cat's eyes, exhilarating. He slid back until the widening of the trunk enabled him to sit up. The cat went back to its digging.

Skydancer braced himself with one hand, his legs looped around the log. He reached for the .45. The pistol caught on his coat and he fumbled with it while trying to maintain his balance.

The cat ceased its digging and watched Skydancer's clumsy attempt to free the gun. Finally getting it loose, Skydancer let go of the log with his other hand. Balanced like a rodeo rider, he brought his elbow down on the log, cocked the weapon and pointed the muzzle toward the far bank.

He was not really surprised to see that the black cougar no longer inhabited it.

"You can't kill me," shouted Skydancer. "You miserable black bastard! You don't know who you're dealing with!"

The triumph in his voice was evident.

Something had happened to Skydancer but he was not aware of it. He moved through the world in a different way now, met each brush with death in the manner of a man very much unlike his old self.

He no longer collapsed in terror at the sudden attack of the black one. Instead, he seemed to accept it as a necessary fact of his existence. It was just something that was, here on Spirit House. Death stalked in the shape of the black one, and unknown to himself, Skydancer now acted like a creature of this world, of Spirit House mountain.

40

By midday Skydancer had covered several more miles. He was walking across a wide expanse of low brush flanked on both sides by low foothills. He held the coat over his left shoulder. The gun dangled loosely in his right hand. He made his way toward a rise where a mass of building-sized boulders towered above him.

He reached the crest of a rise and hesitated, seeing something beyond the top of the largest boulder. He smiled and hurried forward up the rise. Scrambling over broken rocks, he reached the top, panting, and looked down at a familiar object.

It was a telephone pole. And another. Stretching out into the distance as far as he could see. The poles marched across the hills, their wires glistening in the sunlight.

Skydancer laughed.

Still smiling, he turned. Out of the corner of his eye he caught a flash of black and managed to half crouch as the black cougar hit him.

That involuntary movement saved his life. The thickly muscled flank of the night animal hit him solidly in the shoulder, the raking claws slashing the air where his head should have been.

The force of the glancing blow sent him sprawling down the hill. He came to rest on his stomach, on level ground, looking up at the black one, watching him from above like an omen of death.

The gun was on the ground. About halfway up the slope between Skydancer and the cougar.

The dark one hissed and gathered himself to spring.

Skydancer got just to his knees when it jumped.

Whipping his coat up and over his head, he dove sideways. The long deadly body flew at him. As he dove, he whipped the coat over the cougar's death-mask face.

The cat landed beyond him, tumbling in the dirt, its massive head entangled in the coat. Skydancer did not wait for the cougar to free itself.

He stumbled up and ran to retrieve the gun. He fell as he reached the .45. The ground was just too steep. Frantically, he extended his hand, fingers probing for the gun.

He touched it and the motion caused it to slide away. It lodged in a crevice in the rocks. He looked back. The cougar was free of the coat, coming up behind him in a rush.

In an instant, he knew the gun was impossible. Almost without thinking, he jumped to his feet, spinning around to face the charging night beast. It was almost as if he wanted to look into the face of the death he could not avoid.

The cat stopped abruptly.

Skydancer moved slowly to his left, circling back to level ground. The cat looked around as if looking for the gun. Skydancer saw its eyes, and read things in them that made his blood cold.

Skydancer faced it and spoke softly.

"Is it time for me to die, black one? Do you really think you've got me now?"

The cat answered with an earsplitting roar of rage.

The cat moved its head from side to side, hissing. A forewarning of his final attack, the kill.

Skydancer saw it as an answer to his question.

"You shouldn't be so sure of yourself," he said, and there was a strange smile on his face. He pulled Red Hawk's knife from its sheath. He held it out in front of his body with both hands. The cat growled, stopping its final tensing for the last charge.

"Don't be afraid," said Skydancer, and his voice was madly calm, almost peaceful. "I've just got one knife. You've got four sets of them and teeth to match. I'm not scaring you, am I? I hope so, because you're scaring the hell out of me."

Sweat covered Skydancer's face but his hands were surprisingly steady.

The cougar snarled, its tail straight up. It began to circle Skydancer. He moved back, knife up, ready to strike when it attacked.

The black one narrowed its circle until it was within a few feet of Skydancer. Skydancer feigned a thrust at its side. The cat hissed and jumped back, slashing at the air with a taloned paw.

Skydancer smiled. So he could scare the cougar too. The thought made him laugh. He felt strangely powerful in the face of his own inevitable death. He shifted the knife from hand to hand. "Come on now . . . let's finish it!"

The cat coiled like a steel spring, then leapt at him in a light-ning-quick rush. Skydancer sidestepped and slashed at its side as it went by.

"YAYEENAA!" he taunted, lapsing into the forgotten language of his childhood.

The cat screamed and it came to the ground, licking at the thin red line that stained its black coat from front shoulder to back.

Skydancer waved the knife and growled, a poor imitation of his enemy. Even so, the cat backed away as if confused.

Skydancer, not quite sane, was enjoying this combat in some strange way.

He moved toward the black one, brandishing the bloody knife. "Here, kitty, kitty, kitty."

The black one rose, charging its tormentor. Skydancer swung the blade up in a blinding arc at the frothing jaws rushing to seize him.

The cat twisted in midair to avoid the glinting blade and crashed to the ground.

Skydancer cheered the black cougar's pass at him.

"Haneyoka!" Skydancer thought he was talking English.

The black one moved toward him again, but at the sound of his shout, it balked, its coat streaked with dust and blood.

It stopped a yard away, its ugly fangs exposed over yellowed gums.

Skydancer went down on his knees in front of the cat, the knife poised to strike. "The trouble with you," he said to the cat, in the old language, "is that you think you can kill me." He gestured at the cat with the knife and went on speaking very seriously, as if explaining something to a child. "You base your plan of attack on that prem-ise . . ."

He knelt in the dust, instructing the dark one, falling back into English.

"And it's false . . . You see, I can't be killed. I don't know how to die. They don't teach it at Harvard."

He began tracing in the dirt with the point of the knife, eyes somewhere else, the brooding dark one before him almost forgotten.

Skydancer was completely vulnerable. He was like a warrior who lays down his weapons before his enemy, daring him to strike, to prove his own great fighting heart.

He looked up suddenly and the knife again was a weapon in his hand.

"I'm an Indian but you thought I was white. That's why you thought you could kill me. Indians die hard. Plane crashes, madmen with guns, white men with contracts, freezing cold. GODDAMN RADIATION! They can't kill us! So you're just a goddamn black cougar."

He waved the knife in the air.

A low deep sound came from the cat. Skydancer's ravings seemed to confuse the cougar.

The cat edged closer, eyes riveted on the knife.

As the cat moved forward, Skydancer brought the knife up in its face. The cat backed away, hissing in rage.

"You see, you don't have a chance against me. I'm goddamn Crazy Horse. I'm Geronimo. I'm Osceola." He saw the cat looking at the knife. "And this is my war shield!"

Skydancer moved very quickly, stabbing at its side. The cougar was caught off guard. It brought up its forepaws and rolled over on its back. Skydancer stopped in mid-swing, ducked as he twisted the knife in his hand and tapped the cougar hard on the nose with the heavy handle.

The cat screamed and jumped away.

"See. I could have got you right then. But I'm not a bad guy. Isn't that amazing? I don't even hate myself anymore. I'd even let you live if you'd do the same for me. How about it, black beauty? Don't we want to live?"

The cougar spat at Skydancer in rage.

Skydancer shook his head, his eyes glazed, feverish.

"Listen to me. What you need is a rest. You need to get away from it all . . . maybe take a trip to the mountains."

He shook with laughter, almost dropping the knife.

The sudden fit of laughter startled the cat and it cowered back, eyes blazing.

Controlling himself, Skydancer hefted the knife and moved forward. "Okay, white man's school's out. It's time for Indian summer vacation."

He had no idea what he was saying. He felt no terror, only a tidal wave of huge unknowable forces insanely raging within him.

The cat let out a scream and moved its head from side to side, its jaws agape.

It lashed out, lightning quick. Its wicked claws just missed Skydancer's left shoulder.

The scream faded as the cat moved back. It gathered its legs under it and then sprang, twisting in the air as it fell.

The black cougar landed on its back at Skydancer's feet. It spread its legs wide, exposing its chest to Skydancer's knife.

Skydancer swung the knife down, driving it deep into the black cougar's heart. The cougar thrashed on the ground, mortally wounded. The man with the strange ache in his heart had done exactly as the cougar had hoped he would.

Coughing blood, the black cougar's head fell to the hard ground, twitched and shook.

Skydancer stepped back. The knife was stuck in the cougar's chest up to the hilt.

The black one's legs moved spasmodically. The eyes glazed and the cougar stopped thrashing.

It was dead.

It was a magnificent-looking animal, even in death.

The night mover had let Skydancer kill him, as part of its great purpose.

Skydancer didn't know that, probably never would.

Skydancer just stood there in the clearing, staring at the dark one's body. Something swept through him like a fire and it burned away some of the darkness in his soul.

The look of madness passed from his eyes. Something new lurked there. His shoulders lifted, his back straightened and he felt a warm glow of power flowing through him.

There were no words in him to express the strength he felt, the joy of the new power over himself he seemed now to wield. This was not the same Skydancer, lost inside himself, that had crawled out of a wrecked plane and a wrecked life.

This was a different Skydancer . . . a survivor.

41

The mountain had the power to kill . . . the power to heal.

After the man that had killed it was gone, the body of the black one stirred. The black fur on the head rippled, as if an unseen hand stroked it. The fur on the head began to change color, slowly turning lighter and lighter. The color change spread through the fur on the rest of its body.

Patches of the dead cat were already white. The blood matted in its fur melted, turned thin and ran off the coat as if it had been repelled. The long cuts from the knife disappeared, skin closing, leaving no mark or sign that any wound had been made.

The knife slowly began rising out of the deep wound. The knife rose up from the center of the cougar's heart, clean. Not one drop of blood on the blade. It fell out on the cat's belly, slid off and dropped to the ground.

Where once had lain the body of a black cougar, there now lay the body of one snow white.

The legs twitched, began moving. The eyes, a soft yellow, came open. With almost lazy speed, the cat rolled over onto its stomach, then sprang to its feet.

It threw back its magnificent head and its scream echoed across the deep valleys of the mountain.

It stood above the knife that had pierced its heart. The blade of the knife turned into the ground and began to slowly sink. The hilt vanished from sight into the ground.

The snowy cougar turned and headed for the high places, moving in a beautiful, fluid run up the side of the mountain.

It returned to the high places of the mountain that was both its heart and its home.

Skydancer picked up his coat and dusted it off. Going back to the rocks, he stuck one arm into a crevice and retrieved the gun. He didn't really think he needed it. He felt like he could take on the whole world bare-handed and win. Nevertheless, he dropped the gun into his jacket pocket and began his descent down the other side of the hill, angling toward the line of telephone poles.

At the bottom he looked around. The ground was fairly level toward the east, the mountain at his back. He turned around and looked back at the mountain. He no longer thought of it as an alien place, as a nightmare world in which he had been trapped. Instead, it had become the end of a nightmare. It was a place that had tested depths in him he did not know he had and he was almost reluctant to leave the mountain now, for he felt some strange kinship with it.

And yet he had to leave, had to get back home. He turned his back on the mountain and headed along the line of poles, following them back to civilization.

An hour later he saw a house. It was a tumbledown shack set beside a rutted dirt road. The house looked deserted, so he stepped out on the road, heading south, heading home.

As he moved on down the road, it became wider and he could see farms now, a small ranch with a corral and a water tower. He looked skyward as a helicopter flew over the hill in front of him. The aircraft was too far away to spot him and he made no effort to signal it. He just stared at it until it was a small dot in the sky and then walked on.

Skydancer rounded a bend and the dirt road ended abruptly, jutting into a two-lane paved highway. The line of telephone poles forked out and followed the highway in both directions. He walked out to the white line and stood in the middle of the highway, looking first one way, then the other.

To the north the pavement wound uphill, twisting through the foothills toward the mountains. The other way it straightened into a slight downgrade. "Guess this way's as good as any," he said to himself as he started down the grade, walking on the left side of the highway. The sun was warm, and despite the fact that he had taken quite a beating on the mountain, the walking felt good.

A half mile up the road a pickup truck slowed for a curve, then accelerated onward. Solomon Hawk sat behind the wheel, the window on the driver's side open to the sunshine. He listened to the radio as he drove.

". . . at the wreckage site. The only people left are this reporter and a few stragglers from the Federal Aviation Administration who are packing up and getting ready to go home. Two statements made by Norton Harper, head of the search team here, were concise and tragic. He said, 'The FAA lists the cause of the crash as undetermined' and 'Of the one hundred and twenty-six passengers and crew aboard, there were no survivors.' This is . . .'"

Solomon switched the dial to another station and absentmindedly tapped one hand on his knee to the tune of country music as he drove. As he came round another curve in the road, he saw a figure walking away from him on the opposite shoulder.

Solomon eased up on the gas pedal as he approached the man. Strange to see somebody this far out from town, especially afoot.

When Solomon was within twenty-five yards of the man, he stepped on the brake, his hand reaching forward to shut off the radio. The truck rolled to a stop. Solomon stuck his head out of the window and stared at Skydancer.

Skydancer walked slowly, taking in the clear sky, listening to the birds singing. He had not seen the truck pass and he was somewhat surprised to encounter it in front of him on the other side of the road. He looked at it incuriously, then walked right on by, paying no attention to the old man in the cab. He didn't feel ready for people yet. Solomon watched him pass and shook his head. There was something about this man. Something strange.

Solomon shouted, "Hey, you!"

Skydancer turned at the sound of the voice and looked back at the truck. The old man had the door open and was walking toward him.

Solomon looked up and down the road for any sign of another vehicle.

"Car break down?"

"Nope."

A light of recognition came into the old man's eyes. "You must be one of the plane crash people. They been all over the place."

Skydancer grinned. "I guess you might say that."

"Well, you start sightseeing round these mountains, you'll get yourself good and lost. Let me give you a lift into town."

Skydancer's eyebrows went up. "What town?"

Solomon mumbled something that sounded like "Damn tourists," and then pointed in the direction which Skydancer had been walking. "That way about two miles. Come on."

Skydancer shook his head. "No, thanks. I've walked this far . . . Think I'll just try to go all the way." Skydancer smiled. He liked that phrase. All the way.

Solomon studied the smile on the other man's face, then dropped his eyes to study how Skydancer was dressed. Skydancer looked like he'd been run over, face all bruised, clothes torn and soiled with grime. "You look like you been wrestling with a bull and didn't win. You sure you're all right?" There was something very unwhite about this stranger. Solomon wondered if maybe he was some kind of Indian or something.

"Positive," said Skydancer. "In fact, I've never felt better."

"Suit yourself." Solomon turned and walked back to his truck. He felt very strange things about this man. There was something different, something special about this man. Solomon felt uneasy. He got back in his truck and watched the man walking away from him. He thought he would see this man again. He must tell Lianna about this strange man. She would know why this man seemed to be different. Lianna always knew.

He started the truck up and drove past Skydancer. The man waved at him as he went by.

Skydancer walked into a gas station on the outskirts of Northpass. The place looked deserted. He went into the decrepit bathroom in the back and removed his coat.

He splashed water on his face, then leaned into the dirty sink and let the stream of water from the faucet pour over his head.

The cool water refreshed him. He rubbed at his hair with paper towels from a wall holder. It took him the better part of ten minutes to get the grime and dirt off his hands.

He smoothed the droplets of water off his beard and looked into the stained mirror. He looked like a different person. The deep tan that browned his face made him look very unwhite; the ragged beginning of a beard made him look older, somehow stronger.

He laughed to himself as he thought about Pamela's reaction to the new John Skydancer. Hell, maybe he'd keep the beard. It would never be a full growth. Since he was Indian, there wasn't all that much hair to begin with, but there was enough to spoil his junior executive look once and for all. Pamela might like it but her father, Skyler, would hate it. All the more reason to keep it.

For the first time in days he thought about his job. The nagging ache to reach Denver was gone and thoughts of his ordeal mixed back and forth in his mind with such roller-coaster speed it was hard for him to pull out the bits and pieces that were supposed to be important. A lot of things that should have been important no longer appealed to him. He knew that he should find a phone and call his wife, surprise the hell out of her with the news that the reports of his death had been grossly exaggerated. He should probably run outside and grab the first passerby and shout, "I made it! Look at me! John Skydancer, a goddamn survivor!"

But he was hungry. Hell, he had earned it. Food first, then maybe he'd rejoin the rat race. It was the thought of maybe that made him smile.

He pushed open the rest-room door, blinking at the sunlight that washed the mountains. Down the street he saw a cafe sign and made for it, walking in the gutter along a line of parked cars.

People came and went, mostly rescue workers getting ready to go back to Denver. Nobody gave Skydancer a second glance as he mingled with the airmen and forestry people who stood talking in front of the cafe.

Skydancer stopped and looked longingly through the plate-glass window that fronted the restaurant. He had forgotten it took money. His hand went into his pocket, fishing for the last of the candy bars as he watched the people inside eating. Nobody would feed him on credit unless he was willing to tell his story. But for some reason, he really didn't want to. It seemed too private, too special to share. His hand came out of his pocket with half a candy bar wrapped in foil. Caught in the wrapper was a roll of bills. He looked down at it and his eyes went wide.

He unrolled the money, sticky with melted chocolate, and counted it. Almost nine hundred dollars in assorted bills. Part of Red Hawk's loot that Skydancer hadn't known was there. He smiled and wadded up the bills and stepped through the restaurant door. He wondered how much food one could buy with nine hundred dollars.

The interior of the cafe was crowded with rescue workers having dinner. A long bar ran the length of one wall. There were booths along the windows and Skydancer seated himself at one, the smell of food tantalizing him. He picked up a menu and his hands shook as he read off the list of things to eat. He could have eaten anything at that point.

He was startled when a voice said, "What'll it be?"

The waitress was a fortyish matron doing her damnedest to look twenty and failing miserably.

"Can I have one of everything?"

"Look, buddy," she scowled, the purple eye makeup giving her a hobgoblin look, "I ain't got time to fool around. You wanna order?"

Skydancer looked at the menu while the waitress fidgeted impatiently. "Okay. Bring me a steak, the thickest you have."

She scribbled on the pad in her hand. "That'd be the Maneater's Cut, six seventy-five."

"And french fries, lots of french fries. A pot of coffee and ask the cook to fry up three eggs, sunnyside up, and drop them on the steak."

"I dunno. That'd be extra."

Skydancer took a ten-dollar bill from his pocket and pressed it in her hand. "Just do it, okay?"

Her frown was replaced by a crooked smile. "Whatever you say!" She waddled away toward a table that held several coffeepots on burners. Returning, she set a cup and one pot on his table and winked at Skydancer.

When she brought the meal he attacked it with the same vigor and purpose the Japanese visited on Pearl Harbor. The steak was overdone and the coffee lukewarm but somehow he didn't notice. When he had cleaned the plate he ordered half a pie. The waitress openly stared at him. She shook her head but said nothing.

He slid a twenty under the plate and rose, walking to the door. "Anyplace around here a guy can get a shower and a bed?" he asked the waitress, busily setting up another table.

"Down the street about two blocks and turn right. Only motel on that block, so you can't miss it. Most of these rescue people'll be checking out since they got all the bodies down from the mountain. Shouldn't have much trouble grabbing a bunk."

"Thanks."

As he opened the door to leave, she said, "If you're looking for company, I get off in a couple of hours."

Skydancer winked at her and stepped outside. Feeling like a new man, he strolled the streets of Northpass, following the waitress's directions. He was about to turn where she had indicated when his gaze wandered to the field beside the general store.

People were loading canvas bags into a line of waiting trucks and a white-frocked official stood talking to a man and woman. Skydancer strolled into the field and mingled with the workers, fascinated by the long rows of bodies.

He stood and watched the activity and as he did a man in a forestry uniform called to him, "Hey, buddy, lend a hand, huh?"

The man struggled with a bag, trying to lift it onto the back of an Air Force six-by. Skydancer leaned down and grabbed an end, hefting the heavy load aboard. A red tag was attached to the foot of the covered corpse and he glanced at it. It read, "Male cauc., massive facial and torso damage."

Skydancer jumped, recognizing the face through the plastic.

It was Red Hawk.

"Thanks," said the ranger.

Skydancer nodded and the ranger walked off. As Skydancer turned away from his finished task, he came face to face with Pamela and Michael as they walked away from Martin Lusky, the medical examiner.

Skydancer recognized Michael as the tennis pro from his country club, the one who had been giving Pamela such expensive tennis lessons.

They were engaged in an argument and for a few seconds he did not recognize them. When he did he could not believe his eyes. They embraced with the clinging familiarity of lovers. He started to speak but the words stuck in his throat.

Skydancer was directly in their path and Michael was half turned toward Pamela. He bumped into Skydancer.

"Excuse me," he said offhandedly as he went on by, holding Skydancer's wife by the arm. Her glance played across Skydancer's sun- and weather-roughened face without recognition.

She said to Michael. "Let's get drunk and make love all day."

"I'll break your back!" boasted Michael.

"Promises! Promises!" she said sarcastically.

They were half a block away before Skydancer could move. His legs felt stiff and he could hardly walk. He started after them. He was stopped by a voice from behind.

"Quite a pair those two."

The man in the white medical coat had seen the look on Skydancer's face as he came up beside him. Skydancer turned, dazed. "What?"

"You noticed too, huh?" said Martin Lusky, the medical examiner, gesturing after the couple with his clipboard. "Her husband was aboard the 727. Says they came up to reclaim the body. Crap!"

Skydancer had a hard time understanding what was being said to him. Lusky nodded and went on as if he were talking to a colleague. "You ask me, they just want to make sure he's dead so they can collect the insurance or start a fat lawsuit. Look at that guy, will ya? He's practically carrying her tongue in his pockets. Poor bastard she married doesn't know how lucky he is to be dead. Ain't love grand!"

Skydancer just stared, feeling something dying inside him.

Lusky went on.

"They walk away with a fortune and the poor bastard of a husband probably ends up in an unmarked grave. That's justice for you, I guess."

"I thought it was finished," said Skydancer.

"Just about," replied Lusky, assuming Skydancer meant the loading of the bodies. "We get this bunch down and we can close shop. The fly-boys'll be running choppers back and forth to the crash site for a few days 'til the FAA puts a wrap on it, but as far as we're concerned, it's all over. One hundred and twenty-six, present"—he gestured over the field—"and accounted for."

Skydancer finally heard him. He cocked his head and whispered. "All of them?"

"Well, counting the three air crew, that is. Got thirty-six Jane and John Does we may never put a name to, but we'll issue all the death certificates . . . Say, you okay?"

"Huh? Yeah, I'm fine." Skydancer's eyes were glazed and he had difficulty maintaining his balance. He fought to hear over the loud ringing in his ears.

"Well, looks like we're about through here. Why don't you take off?"

Skydancer shook his head. "I have something to do first."

He left the medical examiner standing in the middle of the field. As he walked in the direction Pamela and Michael had taken, he fingered the cold steel of the .45 in his pocket.

42

The sun was setting as Skydancer walked toward the motor court. A fragment of the old John Skydancer stirred within him.

He spoke aloud as he walked. "What are you going to do?"

"I'm gonna tell them I'm alive, that's what."

"Bullshit."

"Well, what else can I do?"

"You can kill them."

"No."

"Yes, you can. It's easy. You just knock on the door and when he opens it you let him get a good look at you before you pull the trigger. Can you imagine the surprise on their faces?

"Yeah."

"Then you kill yourself. You kill yourself because she tried to make you into something you never were. She lied to you, used you, made your whole life a lie. You kill yourself after you kill her."

"No! I love her."

"Yes. You kill her because she doesn't love you. Never loved you. She used you. The whole white world used you. They both used you. Now you've got them both together. You've got the gun. Just follow your instincts."

"I can't."

"You will. You must."

"And then what?"

"Then you put the gun in your mouth and pull the trigger. That's the only way it will ever be all over."

"Won't work."

"Why not?"

"Don't you remember what happened on the mountain. It really happened, you know. I can't be killed."

The voices in his head wouldn't be stopped.

Skydancer came up on the back of the motor court and moved into the brush that lined the rear of the building. He moved stealthily along the edge of the parking lot until he was just a few feet from the long row of windows.

Taking the gun from his pocket, he cocked it and crouched low against the peeling paint.

He crawled along under the windows, lifting his head to peer into empty rooms. The fourth window showed a shaft of light through its faded curtains. He got down on his hands and knees and raised his head slowly up to the sill.

The curtains were uneven and through a crack he could make out the bed with a doorway next to it. Pamela was on the bed. She lay back against two pillows and was talking to someone Skydancer could not see.

He raised the pistol and pressed the muzzle against the window glass.

Michael came out of the doorway next to the bed, naked. He had just come from the shower and was toweling his wet body. Skydancer watched the well-muscled torso shake under the strokes of the towel.

Michael tossed the towel away and settled into the bed beside Pamela. He kissed her and his arms went around her.

The sheet fell away and she pressed her body, fiercely and passionately, against him. Skydancer had seen enough.

Skydancer forced himself to rise, a blank expression on his face, and walked to the woods on the other side of the parking lot. He went a few yards, then fell to his knees. Crawling forward into the brush, he pulled his limp body behind a tree and hugged his knees to his chest. He spent the night there, wrapped in the misery of the old John Skydancer.

When the first rays of sunlight touched his face, it was calm. He did not move until he heard the door of Pamela's motel room open and the sound of a trunk lid lifting. Then he crawled out onto a hill overlooking the parking lot.

Michael was putting luggage into the back of a rental car.

Skydancer watched him as he set a briefcase in the trunk and closed the lid. As he did, Pamela emerged from the room, purse in hand, smiling. Skydancer sighed as he watched Michael move with her to the door of the car.

They were on the side of the vehicle facing the rise and Skydancer brought the gun up, centering the sights on Pamela's head.

The hill was only a few feet above the parking lot, but to Skydancer it seemed as though he was watching the scene from a mountaintop. He looked down at the tiny figures only yards away, his eyes blank, face expressionless.

He felt more than heard the sound of the first shot as the pistol recoiled in his hand. Detached, through a red-filmed haze, he watched the first slug take Pamela above the right eye.

His eyes glazed over as she did a slow-motion pirouette, spinning as her hair and blood splattered the side of the car.

He thought he saw an expression of horror on Michael's face as the man turned to watch her fall against the side of the car, then bounce into the parking lot.

Skydancer did not hear the next shot at all, but he saw Michael raise his hands, palms outward, to protect himself. He saw the red stain take shape on Michael's outstretched palm. Skydancer saw the bullet move through the hand and slam into the man's chest. He saw Michael double over and fall to the ground in a pool of spreading blood.

Skydancer's eyes went out of focus and he stared down at a patch of snow on the ground to regain his composure. Suddenly, he laughed. But it was a different kind of laugh. The dream dissolved.

Skydancer pressed the gun into the snow and scraped more snow over it until it was covered up.

Then he rose and walked down into the parking lot.

As his feet touched the cement, Michael smiled at Pamela and opened the car door for her.

She got in and Michael walked around the car, hefting the last bag. Michael noticed the bearded man on the edge of the lot and nodded a good-morning. Then he tossed his suitcase in the back seat and slid behind the wheel.

Skydancer walked toward the car as Michael started the engine. He stopped a short distance away as the car backed and pulled out. He watched the car swing out on the highway and accelerate away. They were sitting very close together in the car.

Skydancer smiled and raised his right hand in the air. "Screw you both, you deserve each other!"

He felt great. He felt like he had been wanting to say that all his life. His eyes were steady and he had never felt more alive.

John Skydancer realized at that moment he was something he had never been before. Free.

He turned and walked down the road in the opposite direction. Occasionally he stuck his thumb out at a passing car. He had no idea where he was going; it was enough that he was going.

He drank in the beauty of the clear blue sky. Funny how long it had been since he had noticed how pretty a clear blue sky could be.

John Skydancer is dead, he thought to himself as he walked. Officially dead. A John Doe killed in a plane crash. His hands touched his pockets. I've got almost nine hundred dollars in my pocket and a clean slate. I'll find a new name and a new life.

He whistled, felt like kicking up his heels. He had never felt so powerful in his entire life. He stuck his thumb out at a car. To his surprise, it stopped, a sleek convertible. A honey blonde sat behind the wheel. She was absolutely gorgeous.

"You must have been with the rescue teams?" she said. "I'm a reporter, finished up here, heading for L.A. Going my way?"

Skydancer shook his head. "No. I'm going my way."

The blonde shrugged and started to put the car in gear, looking a trifle bored. "Suit yourself."

"However." Skydancer opened the door and got in.

"Change your mind?" she asked, putting the car in gear. She looked him over. There was a rugged, individualistic look to him. She found him very attractive.

"Not me," said Skydancer, settling back in the seat.

The car headed west.

Skydancer looked back over his shoulder, catching a final glimpse of the mountain at his back before they disappeared behind the horizon. He'd left the old John Skydancer on that mountain back there. And good riddance.

"How far are you going?" she asked him.

"All the way. I'm going all the way," he said. "To the top of the mountain, to the end of the road, to the edge of the world, to . . ."

"A motel for the night?" she suggested. "Is that on your list of all the ways? I need to sleep in a real bed tonight. You could make this trip to L.A. real interesting."

Skydancer frowned, the mountain on his mind. He glanced over at her and she gave him one of those looks, the kind of look Pamela used to give him. Suddenly he wanted to be outside, to be out in the open air.

Skydancer counted on his fingers. "Funny you should mention that," said Skydancer. "That seems to be on the bottom of my list of all the ways. Pull over, let me out."

"Suit yourself," she said grimly, pulling the car over.

Skydancer got out slowly and turned to thank her. She muttered "Bastard" at him before he could speak and hit the gas, speeding away. He stood there and watched her go.

Skydancer turned around and looked back toward Spirit House mountain. Suddenly he missed it, wanted to go back to it. It was as if it contained a part of himself. He started walking back. A man with no name and a mountain for a heart.

A mile away, the old man and the old woman sat in the shade of the battered pickup truck.

Lianna smiled, feeling the breeze on her face. "He's coming, Solomon, as I told you he would."

Solomon nodded. "I've made a place for him in the house, where the one we no longer speak of was. I hope he will be happy with us."

Lianna sighed, leaning into the wind. "He will not be happy but it will be enough to be free. We can teach him about the mountain and its ways, and the ways of our people who live in its shadow."

"But are you sure he will accept us? He was strange when I met him, so strange, like he did not really walk on this earth," said Solomon, his eyes staring down the road in the direction they expected him to come.

Lianna smiled with the wisdom of one who does not so much see as know. "You know I know, old man. I see into his heart, as I see into yours. He may not be happy but he seeks his beginnings. We are his people now and the mountain is his heart."

The mountain towered above them. On its slopes high above them, a snow-white cougar stood on a ledge, its eyes on a figure walking in the far distance. The cougar snarled once, turned, ran across the snow and disappeared in the trees. There were no foot-prints in the snow to mark its passing.

Skydancer's eyes were on the mountain. Every step took him closer.

He was going home.

ABOUT THE AUTHOR

Born Ft. Wayne, Indiana, 1950. Full-blood Cherokee father. Mother white. Has been living alternately for the last thirteen years in North Hollywood, California, and Europe. Has had bestsellers in England, Germany, and Holland. His novels, children's books, short story collections, and books of poetry have been widely translated in over fourteen languages.

Under twelve different pen names, he has written more than twenty-six screenplays for film and television, including work for directors like Polanski, Altman, and Mark Robson. He has also directed films and episodic television as well as a number of plays. He has several plays in rehearsal across the country.

He has now fled loathsome Los Angeles, for the relative sanity of almost anywhere else on the East Coast. He has no intention of going back.

He has said, "I came to Hollywood with a thousand bucks and no experience. I left forty-eight thousand dollars in debt and with too much experience. I was lucky to get off so cheaply!"

When asked in a CBS television interview what he wanted out of life as a playwright and an Indian, he said, "As a playwright, only that the visionary world of the Amerindian takes its rightful place in the theatrical sun. As an Indian, there is not too much I want out of life, except maybe someday, a good pickup truck."

Had he been a little more quick-witted, he might have asked for a good pair of cowboy boots too.